JUSTICE AND HER BROTHERS

By Virginia Hamilton

GREENWILLOW BOOKS
Arilla Sun Down
Justice and Her Brothers

MACMILLAN PUBLISHING CO., INC.
The House of Dies Drear
M. C. Higgins, the Great
The Planet of Junior Brown
Time-Ago Lost: More Tales of Jahdu
The Time-Ago Tales of Jahdu
Zeely

THOMAS Y. CROWELL CO.
W. E. B. Du Bois: A Biography
The Writings of W. E. B. Du Bois

HARPER & ROW
Paul Robeson: The Life and Times
of a Free Black Man

Justice and Her Brothers

VIRGINIA HAMILTON

GREENWILLOW BOOKS
A Division of William Morrow & Company, Inc.
New York

Copyright © 1978 by Virginia Hamilton
All rights reserved. No part of this book may be reproduced
or utilized in any form or by any means, electronic or
mechanical, including photocopying, recording or by any
information storage and retrieval system, without permission
in writing from the Publisher. Inquiries should be addressed
to Greenwillow Books, 105 Madison Ave., New York, N.Y. 10016.
Printed in the United States of America   First Edition

1   2   3   4   5   6   7   8   9   10

Library of Congress Cataloging in Publication Data
Hamilton, Virginia.   Justice and her brothers.
Summary: An eleven-year-old and her older twin brothers
struggle to understand their supersensory powers.
[1.   Brothers and sisters—Fiction.   2.   Twins—Fiction.
3.   Fantasy]   I.   Title.   PZ7.H1828Ju   [Fic]   78-54684
ISBN 0-688-80182-X   ISBN 0-688-84182-1 lib. bdg.

For William Hamilton
and Kenneth Hamilton, Jr.

1

Might as well be the same day as yesterday, she thought. Who's to say it's not?

Pouting her displeasure, she sidled through limp and quiet rooms. Sun baked the east and south windows of her home in a blinding yellow glaze from morning until late afternoon. All of the windows were raised and rested on small wood-framed screens that let in the slightest air movement from outside. But steady breezes seemed to have disappeared with the endless heat wave. She was positive it would never rain again, and she decided this morning on leaving the filmy summer curtains closed.

"You can see through them just as well," she told herself, "and even feel the heat outside, too."

Sun scorched away as strong as ever.

Her dad once telling her, "A fella's prisoner to heat when he's dang fool enough to build square in the middle of a flat, dusty field."

Talking about the house they now lived in and the fellow who had built it.

"Why'd you buy it from him, then?" she'd wanted to know.

" 'Cause I'm no better than he is," her dad had said. " 'Cause I can't get over that view down the field, either."

That had sure tickled her and she'd laughed her head off.

Her dad telling: "I do like all that space between me and the neighbors, even when I sometimes fear the field will explode with fire from sheer hot weather. But some nights —I know you've seen it, Tice—the fireflies get to hovering in there and the next thing you know, that field is a haven a blinking stars."

She had nodded in agreement. "But you like that old hedgerow clear on across the west property," she'd asked him. "Don't you just like it the best of all?"

Her whole family knew how much she cared for the hedgerow.

"Even better than the field a stars?" she'd questioned him.

"Oh, but sure, Tice," her dad had said. "That's the truth you are talking about right there. All of those twisting osage trees were just made for the finest sunsets this side of paradise.

"Every evening forever," her dad, going on, "sun'll go down behind our own, very own hedgerow—I picture him a bright-eyed old fella sleeping it off. And never once snagging his crimson-and-gold undershirt on them sticker branches as he slips on down below the horizon."

This last had caused her to squeal with the giggles. Now the memory of it dissolved the pout and made her grin as she entered the parlor of her home and sat down a moment in her father's easy chair.

Called Ticey or simply Tice by all in her family and in the neighborhood, her real name was Justice. "Justice is as Justice does" was something she told herself quite naturally nearly every day. She liked being Justice and did not find the name odd or strange unless some stranger came around and commented on it.

Now Justice snuggled in the chair and caught a feeling

of her dad deep within it. She caught a whiff of his Aqua Velva aftershave, which caused her to summon up almost a shape of his joking and teasing. Then came to her a memory of wind swooshing through the side windows of his battered Oldsmobile.

The parlor was mussed from the previous night's use. But not badly so, Justice decided. Newspapers were piled on the green footstool where her dad had left them. There was a black pocket comb fallen at the foot of the sofa. One of her mom's books, *Contemporary Crafts*, lay open on an end table. Balanced half on and half off the same end table was one of her brother's drumsticks.

How long had it been there like that? she wondered.

As she stared at the stick, something came over her like a slow chill. She pulled her legs up against her chest and scrunched deeper in the chair. She had a cold, uncomfortable feeling whenever she was alone and came across something belonging to her brother Thomas, like that drumstick.

Justice flicked her eyes this way and that. All else around the parlor appeared ordinary. The light of sun set the room aglow in corners and on the walls. It was an eerie effect, but not something she hadn't seen before. The house was stifling, as it had been for weeks. But there was nothing odd about sunlight, about heat, at this early hour. Yet, since the summer started, she'd got the notion at times that something deadly strange was going on.

Maybe it just feels different, she thought, with Mom out of the house each day for the first time this summer. No grown-ups around from morning until way late.

She felt a pang of loneliness at being left all day and mostly on her own. Thomas' drumstick caught her eye as, incredibly, it took a slow roll over the edge of the end table. As if someone had toppled it over.

Justice gasped.

Not someone, she thought, some *thing!*

The drumstick had plopped on the floor and lay still.

She began shivering uncontrollably, imagining a thing invisible moving away from the fallen stick to creep up behind her chair.

So real!

The hair on her neck seemed to crawl. Giddy with fear, she tried with all of her mind and will to control herself.

Saying out loud, whispering, "Justice is as Justice does." It seemed to help a little. Putting her thoughts in order helped even more.

"It had to be on the end table since last night," she told herself. "No one's been out here yet this morning, I can tell. So why did that particular drumstick pick the particular minute I am sitting here to roll off the table?

"It didn't *pick*, you dummy," firmly she told herself. "It fell because it fell, that's all. And I happened to be here to see it. Maybe coming in here like I did jarred it some. . . . Sure! It would've fallen whether it was me came in here or not."

So there. It made sense. Just her and the drumstick meeting up with fate.

But a gnawing fear wouldn't go away. Some *thing* she imagined still waited behind her chair. All alone, she realized she'd had the feeling before.

Yes, but never as strong as now, she thought. Before, it had been so vague, like a soft sound, and I had to glance around to see where it came from.

And it came to her, a pure intuition: whatever it was

4

she imagined behind her chair was a part of something strange going on. The whole weird feeling had begun with the summer and being alone in the house with her brothers.

Least, I don't recall the feeling before this summer.

She had an awful urge to turn around and see if something truly was in back of her chair; but, stubbornly, she refused. The feeling of something remained, as did her determination not to look. Vague and formless as it was, she felt it dare her to find it.

Ever so carefully, she got up from her dad's easy chair, forcing herself not to look around. Casually, she slunk across the room and out, moving smoothly down the hall to the dining room. She let her fingers trail gracefully along the stippled yellow wall as though she hadn't a care in the world.

"Something's very weird," she told herself, and then pretended she had not heard.

There were some neighborhood kids and grown-ups, too, who thought Justice's family, even her house, were "weird."

"Because we're set away from all the other houses," she told herself. "That's the reason they think that. I mean, every day and night we are protected by the hedgerow, but able to see all their backyards way down our field. It's what Dad meant by the view from here. You sure do get to know secrets about folks from the view of what goes down in their backyards!"

Justice giggled.

All the junk they pile up and think they are hiding. Fights spilling clear out onto the back porch!

And they can't view us.

She had to smile.

Because, looking up the field, they only get to see this big wood fence around *our* backyard. We are so private at the end of our blacktop road, too. They are public on the street. That's maybe why we're "weird."

But she knew better.

Oh, people are just so boring.

All except for Mrs. Jefferson, and her husband, and her son, Dorian. They were fairly new people in the old neighborhood near farmland, and they lived directly down the field from Justice's home. She visited Mrs. Jefferson and her son quite often because her own mom was never home and she needed someone like Mrs. Jefferson, or at least that age, to be around.

But a lot of other people, other than the Jeffersons, were just so boring.

I mean, she began to herself, they don't get upset when they see a tract of houses just alike. Or a forest of the very same trees. But they have to go and pay all that attention to Thomas and Levi. Phooey!

Thomas and Levi were her thirteen-year-old brothers. And on the outside they were identical.

Seeing the dining room after dawdling down the hall, Justice realized suddenly that she'd better hurry. By the time she entered the room, she was moving fast.

"Tice, where are you off to at this hour?" asked her mom.

"Wha—?" Startled, Justice had known her mom would be there, but, thinking so hard, she'd forgotten.

"I . . . Oh, you *know* I gotta get going," she said, annoyed at having to defend herself at seven-thirty in the morning. Her mom looked bright and shiny without any makeup, Justice noticed, even though there were permanent creases at the corners of her eyes.

"But I still don't know why you have to go," her mom said, "or in what direction you're going."

She had seen her daughter going for the last two mornings since Monday and preparing to go again now. She'd heard from her sons that Ticey returned hours later, looking hot and sweaty but not really any the worse for wear. Tice would stay home for a while at lunchtime, but then would sometimes again disappear for another hour. Suddenly, Mrs. Douglass wondered if the boys were telling her the whole story.

"I told you," Justice was saying, racing around the table to where her mother sat with an open book and a mug of strong Morning Thunder herb tea.

"You didn't tell me anything," Mrs. Douglass said. "And you haven't had your breakfast."

"I don't *want* any breakfast," Justice said. She searched in every corner of the room. She raced into the kitchen to do the same there and ran back to look under the dining-room table one last time. Crawling out from underneath, she accidentally bumped the tabletop. And looked on in shock as Morning Thunder splashed out of the mug.

"Ticey!"

"Mom!" Tea spreading in a brown stain on the tablecloth. "You know I didn't mean to. Where's my jacket—please? Don't you remember where I put it?"

"*I* should remember where *you* throw things?" her mom said. "Here, hand me those napkins."

"You used to remember where I thro—put things, before."

Her mom soaked up spilled tea. Justice helped her roll back the cloth to wipe the table.

"Meaning, I guess, *before* I had to study all the time," Mrs. Douglass said.

"Correct," said Justice, watching her mom make a pile

of soiled napkins. Still on her knees, she peered over the edge of the table at the open book her mom had shoved out of the way of the spill. It was *Lecturas Escogidas* again. She knew what the title meant. It was Spanish for *Selected Readings.*

Her mom was a student at Marks College twenty miles away in some degree-completion program.

When she should have been home to help when Justice needed her to find things, was Justice's opinion on the subject.

Her brothers, Thomas and Levi, thought it great to have their mom away all summer long, from nine in the morning until three and four in the afternoon.

"Think of the devilment you can do," Thomas told Justice one day. He beat his drumsticks on the back of her chair. "I'll keep a list of it to show Mom."

The tone of his voice and those whirring sticks had caused Justice to suspect he would hit her deliberately. She had screamed at him, *"I truly despise you!"* And, unreasonably, she had burst out with, *"If you ever touch my bike . . . !"*

It had made him turn on her, screeching with laughter. Even Levi had had to go laugh at her. But no one could fake screeching and shaking all over quite the way Thomas could.

"You *are* a pickle," he had said. It was the stupid nickname he had thought up for her. "Who'd want a dumb three-speed except a sour pickle?" Pounding his drumsticks so close to her ear she could feel the air move.

Now Justice rubbed her nose back and forth along the smooth dining table. She felt unsettled, nervous, inside.

He dislikes me enough to hurt me, Thomas does, she thought. Oh, phooey on him, and Levi, too.

But she felt uneasy all the same.

As soon as she'd found out that Thomas was planning a special event this coming Friday called The Great Snake Race, she had known what she had to do. This was Wednesday.

Gives me either one of two days, she thought, as a ribbon of fear uncurled along her spine.

Mrs. Douglass had cleared the table of soggy napkins and had sat down again with her book and tea. As she studied, she commenced running her fingers gently through Justice's brown, curly hair. After a moment, she glanced sideways to find Justice staring at her, looking very sour.

"Tice, what is it?" she said. "What's troubling you?"

"Nothing," Justice mumbled. Thinking of her brothers and The Great Snake Race had made her glum and out of sorts. She did like the way her mom fluffed her hair, though. Her mom knew how to make it feel pretty and not at all tangly.

"Do you dislike my going to school so much?" asked Mrs. Douglass.

"No," Justice said. It wasn't a bother that her mom went to school.

But that she's gone for hours and hours, Justice thought. And not here to help. To be on my side from Thomas.

"Shall I have a word with your brothers about calling you Pickle?" her mom asked.

Justice looked surprised. "Why do you have to know so much?" she said, not unkindly.

Mrs. Douglass smiled at her.

Justice stared at *Lecturas Escogidas*. "Guess you don't know everything," she said. "I could read a book that size in two days. It's taking you forever."

Mrs. Douglass laughed. "But it's a study book, Ticey.

You don't read a textbook like this straight through."

"Oh, right," Justice said. "I knew that, but I just forgot a minute. You have to memorize stuff, same as I do."

"Yeah," said her mom.

Justice suddenly looked smug. "Here's what I memorized this week: 'Breathes there the man with soul so dead, Who never to himself hath said, "This is my own, my native land." ' "

" 'The Lay of the Last Minstrel,' " her mom said. "Well, I'll be—are they still teaching that? But you said you just learned . . ."

Justice cut in on her: "And I know 'They have tormented me, early and late, Some with their love and some with their hate. The wine I drank, the bread I ate, Some poisoned with love, some poisoned with hate . . .' "

" 'Yet she who has grieved me most of all,' " Mrs. Douglass broke in on her, looking somewhat astonished at her daugher.

" 'She neither hated nor loved me at all,' " finished Justice.

They were silent a moment as the echo of words seemed to flow about them.

"You didn't learn that in school," finally her mom said.

"Nope," Justice said. "I learned it from Levi. He's always reading slushy stuff like that. When he's up in the cottonwood, I climb up. He's reading out loud and he sees me and says to me, 'Tice, wanna hear? Then keep quiet and listen.' So I hang on a limb and listen as long as I want."

"That's wonderful," said her mom.

"I don't like it much," Justice said. "But I like Levi sometimes. Do you really like memorizing all the time?" she asked.

"Well, it's more that I study until I get to know stuff well. And, sure, I like it. You will, too, I bet, when you grow up."

She felt sleepy from the soft movement of her mom's hand in her hair. But suddenly she leaped to her feet with slightly more drama than was necessary. "I should-a been gone!"

"Should have been— Tice? Where are you off to?"

"Mom, I told you once. I have to practice."

"Practice what?"

"Moth-er, I have to go—can't you remember where my jacket is at?" She didn't need the denim jacket. She knew the day would get blistering hot. But the jacket was familiar, like a second skin, tight and safe.

"Practice what?" Mrs. Douglass repeated. "Maybe you'd better tell me what's going on before you leave the house."

"You never make Thomas or Levi give you a rundown."

"Yes, I do, too."

"Shhhh!" Justice whispered, although her mother had spoken in the same voice as before. "The boys might hear!" she whispered. Why did her mom have to become more difficult with each new morning?

"Then, *what?*" Mrs. Douglass, said, whispering.

"Mom, trust me, will you?"

"Tice, don't sound so old," Mrs. Douglass said in a normal tone. "And you can't use that on me, either."

"Mo-om, I just have to practice something on my bike is all," Justice told her. "It's something Thomas and Levi think I can't do—and that's the utter truth!"

"I only want to know where you go," Mrs. Douglass persisted. "I'm not saying you *can't* go."

"I ride around, over to the playground, and over to the

baseball field," Justice lied. "Not around any cars, don't worry."

"Tice, now listen to me," Mrs. Douglass said.

"Mom . . ."

"I can usually depend on you not to do anything foolish, so don't do wheelies and stunts like that."

"Moth-er! What do you think I am? Girls are different from what you were like as a kid—you know? And probably smarter, and they can do anything boys can do! I could do wheelies by Third Grade, for Chrissakes!"

"No cussing, if you don't mind," said her mom, seemingly unperturbed, although she was impressed by her daughter's ability to express herself. "And no riding double," she added, "it's against the law. Don't ride with no hands down any streets—one slick spot in the road and you've had it."

Save me from mothers! thought Justice.

"You think my jacket could be in the boys' room?" she asked her mom.

"Not to change the subject," Mrs. Douglass said, eyeing her daughter.

Justice thought it best not to answer. Her expression remained as childishly sweet as it could be.

"Dear Ticey, I know all of your tricks by now," her mom said firmly. "I have no idea what you do every minute of the day and I'm not going to pump the neighborhood to find out. Just remember," her mom finished.

"Oh, I remember," Justice said. "How can I forget?" Justice is as Justice does.

She watched as her mom gulped the tea.

"I'm going to be late if I don't get myself together," Mrs. Douglass said. "I did see your jacket in the boys' room,

12

yes," she told Justice. "Tom-Tom hid it up on the encyclopedia shelf. I meant to take it down. . . ."

"Brother!" Justice whispered. Him doing things like that all the time! Another reason I have to win The Great Snake Race. Boy! Only, how in the world do you race snakes?

She ran for the boys' room and stopped dead still at the entrance. How many times had she come into their room in the morning to find something belonging to her, or to wake up Levi? So many she couldn't count them. But this time she hesitated, not moving a muscle.

Why *did* Thomas have to take her things and hide them like that?

She'd seen it as just his way of being funny. But now she realized she might never have found her jacket.

Like he was being mean in earnest.

Cautiously, she tiptoed into the darkened room, counting on her brothers being dead to the world. In summer, Thomas stayed awake half the night watching science-fiction or horror films on TV, when he could find them. And from them he'd learned his sickening, screeching laugh and a lot of different personalities. These he used on Justice and other decent, normal, unsuspecting persons. He pretended he had himself made up certain dramatic characters. But Justice knew he was simply a copy-cat.

On the other hand, her brother Levi was a light sleeper. He couldn't drift off with the television going full blast in the parlor. So he would end up wide awake, watching the films also. He would never tell Thomas to shut the box off. He never complained.

Justice never called her brothers Tom-Tom and Lee, as most of the neighborhood kids did, and as did her mom and dad.

Wonder why I won't? she thought.

She found her hands were trembling. She was standing right next to Thomas' bed. She could see part of his face and his dark, curly hair on the pillow. She heard his breath come in a gentle snore. It took all of her nerve to move, to climb onto the desk chair and then onto the desk in front of the bookcase.

What's wrong with me? There's nothing to be scared of.

But she was, and she quaked inside.

At the far end of the room she glimpsed the round, shadowy forms of Thomas' "instruments of torture," as she called them.

Yuk, she thought. And then: Better keep your mind on what you're doing, too.

She reached above her head as high as she could.

"Darn!" she said, before she thought. And held her breath as Levi stirred on the top bunk. He flung himself over in bed. He caught a glimpse of her as he turned to the wall, and let out a groan.

"Great," he said sleepily. And suddenly he rose up in alarm at seeing her above his head.

Justice smiled brightly. Putting a finger to her lips, she motioned to him to be quiet.

Levi stared at her. He next peered down over the side of his bunk to find that Thomas below him was still deep asleep.

"Oh," he said softly, pulling the covers up again. "What are you doing up there? What time is it?"

"Shhh!" she whispered. "Early. You can go on and sleep. But first will you get my jacket where Thomas put it on the shelf? I can't reach it."

"What?"

14

"Shhh! My jacket, I can't—reach—it!"

Groaning, Levi rose up with a sheet wrapped around him. On his knees, he was tall enough to reach the jacket shoved to the back of the highest shelf.

And handed it to her. "Where you going, anyway?" He spoke softly again.

Shaking her head to dismiss the question, she said nothing as she began her climb back down.

Of her identical brothers, she much preferred Levi, who was more likely to be nice to her. Often he could be kind when Thomas wasn't too close by. Thomas appeared to have a weakening effect on Levi. And since their mom had been in school, Thomas had seemed tense around Justice.

Guess I get in the way of his bad temper, she thought, as she stepped from desk chair to the floor. He and Levi are to look after me this summer, Mom says. To know where I go and to feed me when I'm hungry. I don't mind —they do let me have my way. And if they get to go somewhere, I get to go or one of them has to stay home with me. So phooey on them! So if there's to be a gang and a snake race, I get to be in on it all! So there.

"I know where you're going," whispered Levi from his bunk.

Justice stopped still.

"You're scared if you go with us Friday, you might crack up on the Quinella. You going to practice riding down it!"

"Shut up," Justice whispered back.

"Huh?" It was Thomas. Justice was practically standing in front of him, whispering. "Wh-what is it?" Opening his eyes. He saw Justice and yelled: "G-g-gehhht *outta* h-here!"

She raced from the room.

Brother. "I despise him, I truly do," she told herself,

15

once she was a safe distance away. And shoved her arms into the denim jacket, straightening the collar. She checked the sleeves to see if her arms had grown any longer, something she felt obliged to do each day. Nope. They hadn't. I'll be a shrimp all my life, for Chrissake. The shortest eleven-year-old in the world.

The thought made her both angry and sad.

She returned to the kitchen and her mom on a wave of injured feeling. At the counter, she drank the glass of tangerine juice waiting for her, and avoided looking at her mom. The juice was good and cold, but it did little to ease the hurt Thomas had caused.

Mrs. Douglass studied her daughter's sullen face. She had heard yelling and she surmised it had come from Thomas, since Levi seldom raised his voice. She reminded herself to have a word with Thomas about his ongoing treatment of his sister.

"They look so much alike," Justice said, finally, as she had said so many times before about her brothers, "so why are they so different?"

Mrs. Douglass smiled sympathetically. She knew Justice wasn't really asking. So she stayed quiet while preparing a lunch to take along to school.

The boys were as identical as two peas in a pod, and it was also true they were as different as night from day. They had the same brown eyes and the same arch to their dark brows. Same black, curly hair, same hands and feet, same walk. Levi liked books and would read anything he could get his hands on. He loved music and poetry. However, Thomas led everybody and told everyone what to do and what not to do. All the kids did whatever he told them. He had a highly developed rhythmic and percussive ability. He also had a terrible stutter.

16

Justice looked solemn. Something nagged at her, and slowly she found the words to speak about it.

"I look at one and then the other," she said. "Mom? I get to thinking one of 'em is inside a mirror—do you ever? It's Levi trapped in there, and he can't get out! It's so creepy."

Concerned, Mrs. Douglass crossed the space between them. She wrapped Justice in her arms as a worried look rippled over her features.

Justice felt like a baby standing there holding on to her mom. But, she had to admit, she enjoyed every minute of it. She knew nothing could hurt her, threaten her, with her mom so close.

"Oh, well, Tice," her mom said, "it's easy to imagine all sorts of things. Especially when Tom-Tom and Lee seem so self-contained in their own private realm. Have you ever known two boys to get along so well? But it gets hard keeping things settled down when even adults have to go make up stories."

She chose her words carefully. She didn't want to upset her daughter any further, but she did want Justice to understand exactly what her brothers were.

"We who are their family have to keep in mind certain things," she said.

"Like what?" Justice asked.

"Well, that your brothers don't only look alike, Tice. They also have identical inherited information called genes. They have the same blood group and the same brain patterns. They came from one fertilized egg, just as you did. But the *two* of them came from one egg and it divided into two identical parts. And that's as close as two people ever get to being, feeling, seeing and looking like one another."

Mrs. Douglass took a deep breath, calming herself a bit. Justice wondered why she seemed so excited, and she watched her mom closely.

Mrs. Douglass continued, "You weren't far wrong when you said one was like a reflection of the other. But it shouldn't seem creepy. Because for them it's natural. Their kind are known as mirror identicals."

"Really?" Justice said.

Her mom nodded. "Tom-Tom is left-handed," she said, "and Lee is right-handed. Tom-Tom parts his hair on the right while Lee parts his on the left."

"Right!" Justice said. "I knew that, but I never kind of put it together."

"Well," Mrs. Douglass said, and paused a moment. "I myself have been guilty of thinking there's something odd —you know, I've told you stories. But perhaps odd is normal for them. Just remember that nearly every moment each one has to face the spitting image of himself. Levi once told me it felt like he was seeing himself and someone exactly like himself at the same moment. He said it was like 'feeling double.' And I could almost understand what he meant."

Justice laughed suddenly, and nodded. "Must be like when I look in a mirror. I sometimes can feel myself looking at myself. I'm the reflection, and the reflection is me. I can 'feel' both going on and on forever. Boy, but for Thomas and Levi it must be really weird."

They were quiet a moment. Then Justice said to her mom, "Tell me about them again."

She loved the stories her mom could tell. Funny and sometimes strange things about the boys when they were babies. She pulled away from her mom to lean against the counter.

18

"Tice, I don't think I have the time today," Mrs. Douglass said.

Justice slowly pivoted, turning halfway from her.

"Maybe I should stay home this morning," her mom said, studying her.

Justice peeked around. This was something unexpected —her and her mom together for an entire day, the way they used to be.

"Oh, but I can't, hon, not today. Tice, I'm sorry! There's usually a quiz in the middle of the week. Anyway, I shouldn't miss classes when they charge you an arm and a leg to take them."

She watched her small, dark-eyed daughter suck her fingers.

"Ticey." Mrs. Douglass came over to her. She gently turned her daughter to face her. "You're my favorite girl, you know that, don't you? And your dad's, too. You're the girl we always wanted."

"Mom!" she managed to whisper. Her face flushed and she covered it with her hands as her eyes began to tear. But with great effort she managed to control herself.

"I gotta go," she said, finally. She did not enjoy having her mom leave her, and she felt much better about it when she left the house first, rather than the other way around. Also, she didn't like being home with her mom not there to make it safe.

"You sure you're okay?" her mom said. She peered at her daughter.

Justice hid away her feelings of apprehension. "I'm okay. Bye. See you later, Mother-gator." She gave her mom a quick kiss on the cheek.

Mrs. Douglass gave her a nice one back. "Bye, sweetie. I'll call to check around noon."

19

Well, I won't be here, Justice thought. She paused at the kitchen entrance. "Can't you tell me just the one?" she said. "About what happened when you'd call one of them for something?"

"What?" But quickly Mrs. Douglass understood what Justice was referring to. "I don't have the time, Tice, I really don't."

"Yes, you do, too. I don't care if you tell it fast."

"But you know that story," Mrs. Douglass said.

"I know I know it. At least, I do when you tell it. Just tell it—please?"

Mrs. Douglass sighed. "If that'll get me to school faster . . ."

Grinning, Justice ran to stand before her.

"Okay, here it is," her mom began. "The boys were about three years old when I happened to notice something. I'd call out for Thomas to come to me. In summer, the screens would be in like now. He usually would be outside and he'd hear me and he'd come running. Well, I'd call for Levi the same way. You'd find him either in or out with Thomas—he never seemed to prefer indoors or outdoors, he was satisfied as long as Thomas was with him. Anyhow, I'd call for Levi, and Thomas would come to me. I'd tell Thomas to tell Levi I wanted him. And back would come Thomas by himself. If I wanted Levi for something, I'd have to go get him. Otherwise, I'd get Thomas every time."

Justice stood there, fascinated. "Age four," she said.

Without a pause, Mrs. Douglass continued. "When the boys were four years old, there was a slight change. I'd call for Thomas and he would come. I'd call for Levi, but I would get Thomas *pretending* to be Levi. Or I would call for Levi and both boys would show up. That's it."

Justice had listened with rapt attention. She knew the story by heart and she still loved it. But, for some reason, this time she had to know more.

"What does it mean?" she asked softly.

Her mother shrugged. "I think probably they were just trying to sort out who they were," she said. She sighed and hurriedly turned back to her work at the sink, where she began rinsing lettuce for sandwiches.

"Well, do you think they've sorted it out by now?" Justice asked. And then sucked in her breath as a sudden inspiration came to her. She didn't wait for a reply, but said, "You know what *I* think? Age three or age four, you always got Thomas when you called. But you never got Levi of his own free will—right?"

Her mom didn't answer. With the water running and her mind on getting to school, she might not have heard.

So Justice went on her way. She did have her own business to attend to. She swept through the house in strides much too long for her short, muscular legs. Walking as if she were seven feet tall made her sneakers squeak importantly on the hardwood floors. Thomas had repeatedly warned her that sneakers made black marks on the paste wax.

"Liar—liar!" Justice had singsonged right back at him. Just the other day, too.

By the time Mrs. Douglass realized that her daughter hadn't had anything substantial to eat, it was too late and Justice was out of the house. Outside, thoughts of her sometimes peculiar brothers and even her mom receded for Justice as she stood in the shade of the front porch.

"Oh, nice. Neat!" she said.

The sun beat down on grass and driveway. It was the sort of glaring light that made their white house with black trim look brand new.

"Bet there's not a cloud." She leaped from the porch out over the steps onto the short walk to the driveway. She saw that the sky was a forever blue. Just the kind they say in Ohio country is a California sky. Her dad liked to say that the forever blue with no moisture must arrive from westward by hopping a dawn freight train of the B&O Railroad.

There were a few clouds, Justice noticed. White, fluffy things, hardly moving, like sleeping puppies of the sky.

"It'll get hotter'n hell," she cussed to herself, "but I'll be back home by then."

Unlocking her bike at the edge of the steps, she afterward tucked the chain-lock key on its cord under the neck of her T-shirt. And hopped onto her bike, as agile as a cat on a fence. Bike-riding three-speeds thrilled her and took most of her time and energy. Justice rode all of the streets in town—once in a while with two or three girls from school. She'd ridden some distance out along country roads, past farmhouses and long lanes, all by herself.

Best of all, she liked biking on her own, to stop wherever she pleased. But today she had no time to free-wheel. Like yesterday and the day before, Justice had sure, awful work to do.

2

From home, she took the gravel lane fast on her three-speed, risking a slide on sharp stones. She loved the way the lane and her house were situated at the end of a narrow blacktop road called Union. At the entrance of the property was an enormous cottonwood tree, at the top of which Levi often sat reading his books. The cottonwood had to be the biggest tree in the whole world; certainly bigger than any Justice had seen. Slowing to pass it, she looked up from under thousands of leaves and tens upon tens of stretching branches.

You grand, you tall woman, she thought. Better than a hundred and fifty years old, I bet.

Levi had said the cottonwood was older than a century, but he hadn't said it was a woman.

Little kids of long ago making toys of your leaves.

He'd told her that Indians of past centuries had to have lived close to the tree. "Find a cottonwood," he'd said, "and you'll find fresh, running water, good for cooking and drinking."

Maybe back then, she thought. But there was no running water on the property now.

Cottonwoman forever stands alone. You'll find a black walnut tree nearby to stand as tall as she.

Levi had explained how the scarce black walnuts grew wherever cottonwoods and sycamores stood. Sure enough, a black walnut, brittle-limbed with age, stood to the side of the field they owned.

High up in the cottonwood, leaf upon leaf commenced a rustling. On the base branches, leaves hung limp and lifeless. Suddenly the whole height of the tree was caught in a gentle current of air.

Well, woman, pull on your shawl, it's just so cool up there!

Justice laughed, screamed with the giggles and tore down the blacktop Union Road. At a wide street called Dayton, she paused to look both ways, then wheeled across it onto Tyler Street, which would take her clear across town.

Justice used each of her speeds to see that they all worked properly. Squeezing the hand brakes, she brought the bike nearly to a standstill. Before stopping completely, she pulled on the pedals and raced ahead once again. She speeded, non-stop or -skid, clear to Xenia Avenue, where she waited for a year for the light to change to green. For cars to stand at attention for her. Finally, the light changed. She glided safely across the avenue, still on Tyler where it narrowed with tight, sleepy houses on either side.

"Not a lot of space for houses over here," she said to herself. "Not like the open field where I come from."

She pretended she had come to town on the B&O line like the freight-hoppers of years ago that her dad once told her about. They had come undercover of the forever sky, fleeing a great dust bowl—something Justice couldn't quite picture. But she noticed there sure were a lot of freight-hoppers around today. Boy and girl hoppers carrying the books they'd read on the long B&O ride from California. They hurried along, crossing Tyler Street and turning onto Xenia Avenue.

Actually, they were students going to summer school.

Set.

Swiftly riding, she released ⊁the handlebars and hand brakes to grasp the seat beneath her. Simultaneously, she removed her feet from the pedals to stretch her legs up and stiffly forward until they rested on the handlebars. With the slightest lean, she started the bike turning in circles in the road.

Go!

Justice had slid from the seat onto the crossbar. Letting go of the seat, she leaned her back over it. And she had speed enough for four good circles around in the road. With arms held out to the sides, she might have been a child asleep on a comfortable couch.

There—yeah!

Posed and balanced to perfection. On the last one and one half circles around, she lifted her arms straight above for the ear-splitting applause.

You wish! was her fleeting thought.

She had to struggle to get her feet down and scoot back on the seat before the bike fell over on its side. Not a second too soon, she leaped off and caught the bike in an awkward crouch.

Have to figure a way to get down more graceful, she thought. But not now. Anyway, it's a better trick than anything I've seen boys do.

Practicing the trick was not what she was here for.

"Best get off of the road," she told herself. She pedaled a short distance through a part of the road that was even and ordinary. So began the straight-out Quinella, a hot country road on the way to farmland, small towns and nowhere.

But on the right was an expanse of countryside. In the forefront, next to the road, was a field with a barbed-wire

27

fence. Here Justice stopped the bike. The fence was as far as she had gone on Monday and Tuesday. Today she would go the rest of the way. This she had promised herself.

First, she worked to get her bike through three barbed wires, which was what the fence consisted of. Sliding the bike between the lowest and middle strands, she took care that the barbs didn't puncture a tire or scratch the paint.

Whew! And once the bike was through, she held the strands apart and gingerly stepped in, one leg at a time.

Justice hid her bike in the tall weeds along the side and headed on, the blue sky for company.

Well, *like* a field, she thought as she walked away from the road and fence behind her. She had no idea how long a boundary the fence made, or where it ended. There was no sign of it ahead of her. The place like a field opened up, going on and on, with grand shade trees ahead of her and to one side. Within those trees was heavy shadow growing deeper until it appeared to be darkness. And shade, forever trapped under the trees, was as black as night against the open land where she walked bathed in sunlight.

Oh, don't make me go in the shade by myself.

Talking to herself. But she knew what she must do. Sooner or later, she must enter the shade and face the hard work.

Trudging in sunlight through tall weeds, Justice soon had spiny burrs stuck to her pants legs. She didn't mind them. Always, she seemed to have some weed mark or grass stain on her clothing. Her mom said she was as countrified as she could be. Better than to be citified, Justice would say. And her mom saying right back, Well, listen to her!—whatever that was supposed to mean.

Now Justice heard the sound of water rushing. She smelled the river odor and believed it must be the smell of moss rotting, of edgewater drying up along the banks because of the lack of rain. Distasteful, stale, it flowed over her minutes before she came face to face with the Quinella Trace.

Here, right on the water, everything burned with heat and brimmed over with moisture. The sun had taken up the river water on the air and spread it over the surrounding land. And here even the forever sky from California was a misty blue.

"Breeder weather," Justice whispered to the light of sky.

Her dad often said that. Squinting into just such misty air, he told how such moisture and heat would eventually breed thunderheads of rainstorms.

So far, he's dead wrong, Justice thought. She couldn't get it out of her head that it would never rain again.

And wondered just a moment what her dad might be doing at this moment. Thinking about him easily, no pain. She never missed him the way she did her mom. Maybe because he had gone off to work for as long as she could remember. And by six-thirty in the morning.

Justice squinted purposefully. White fluff clouds had grown a mite bigger, closer, but there was nothing about them to suggest thunder and rain.

She strode on, sweeping her feet in a sideways motion to press the weeds down. In sunlight, she needn't worry about what could lie hidden at the roots. She kept her eyes a pace ahead of the movement of her feet. And before she had expected it, she was standing on the bank of the Quinella Trace.

"Well." Weeds had not parted to show her that the river lay before her. They ceased to grow about a foot and a half from the edgewater.

She was standing on the low bank that was a mud flat

29

in proper weather. Now it was bone dry and a smooth slate gray. Bending, she dug at something white almost buried in the powdery earth. Got it out. It was a near-perfect skeleton of a tiny fish. Examining it a moment, but letting it loose as her eyes fixed on the black-water Trace.

Means to follow lines. Trace, she thought, as, standing here, she had thought before.

Or to disappear and—leave barely a clue!

This last was a new discovery in her mind.

If you did leave a clue, you'd leave a "trace." That's why it's named Trace?

She began to puzzle it out.

The black water could have dried up, with just a trace left where the water once had been. So someone named it Trace.

Centuries later, the black water had flowed again.

Why didn't they change the name to Filled Up, or something?

Trace was what it used to be and still is. Maybe for a thousand years! But only seventy or a hundred years of being the *Quinella* Trace.

"I don't know," Justice said softly.

Her dad had told her that, long ago, boats had been raced on the river. And she'd thought Quinella was a person's name until some boy said it was a betting game. But for sure she knew that the Quinella Trace was the blackest water anybody'd ever seen. Nobody, not one kid she knew, had any idea why.

Wasn't water supposed to be blue like the sky? They all thought so. There was the blue reflection of sky in it, but the water itself stayed fear-dark. Kids used to wade in it until a story got started around. The kind of darkness tale that someone like her friend Mrs. Jefferson, down their field, might think to tell. Mrs. Jefferson told lots of things that Justice had a way of forgetting. But she knew the story told about the Quinella was true.

Levi sure proved it, too.

The sound and the flowing sight of the black water made Justice shiver. Yet she was burning warm, standing so still by the edgewater. Whining sounds of insects were close around. Gnats were worrisome, trying to nest in the wet creases as she squinted her eyes. She mashed them with her fingers and rubbed them away. Her hands felt hot and clammy on her face.

Maybe if I stick my feet in just once to cool off.

But she hadn't the nerve.

'Cause they come so fast on you. The slimy devils! she thought. Maybe something *forms* them as you set foot in the water. And *warns* them you are stepping in.

Glancing all around, Justice thought about leaving.

Run away and forget it!

And thought again about sticking her feet in.

"This whole Quinella place is just so devilish!" Saying it low on her breath seemed to calm her. "I'm not gonna put my feet in, not on your life I'm not!"

Angry at not being foolish enough or brave enough to wade in the warmish black water. It had been right here at the Trace that something awful had happened to Levi.

Never to forget it, either, never in my life.

As she thought about the incident, something dawned, more important than the memory of it.

Their dad had brought them down here to fish—her, Thomas and Levi. She had been about eight years old. Not that long ago. Thomas never could get enough of good fishing, and neither could her dad. Levi liked swimming, and Justice had felt at home searching the edgewater for flat stones to mark with her initials.

Levi had waded to his waist in the water; then he had plunged flat out on his stomach.

"Feels like lukewarm soup!" he'd shouted to them.

"You've had experience swimming in lukewarm soup," her dad had shouted back, laughing.

It was the sequence of what had happened next that now loomed out of the memory, like pictures from a scrapbook suddenly spotlighted.

Not another word had been spoken. Levi had looked peculiar. Thomas hadn't been watching Levi swim, but suddenly he had dropped his fishing rod. Thomas had slowly got to his feet, his mouth hanging open, as Levi swam toward shore.

Like clear snapshots torn from an album and held close to intense light.

Justice stood absolutely still now at the edgewater, transfixed by pictures framed crystal clear and perfect in her mind's eye.

Levi wading out of the water, not aware of anything wrong but maybe sensing something was wrong because of the strange way Thomas was staring at him. Their dad leaping up as if something had stung him hard, gaping at Levi also.

Levi had begun running frantically around and around. He had started screaming in this terrifying wail.

Fat, slimy worms had covered his chest and back. Black, blood-sucking leeches all over his legs. The river had to have been full of them. They'd been the most scary, the most devilish things to see.

Their dad had tried to pull them off Levi. But the leeches had clung to his skin as they sucked his blood. Awful for her to think about even now.

Their dad had hurried with matches, lighting two, three at a time for the bigger leeches. Burning the beasts off Levi. Levi's body jerking, shivering. Him screaming the worst forlorn sound the whole time.

"Never to forget it," Justice told herself. "I can still smell them slimy beasts burning. And see 'em curl up like dry crisps and fall."

Not only the memory. That's not all of it, she thought. But the way Thomas had dropped his fishing rod.

The funniest thing!

Dropping it and getting to his feet. Staring at Levi before they ever knew there were going to be leeches all over him.

Justice jumped away from the edgewater, startled by the suggestion of her own mind.

She began following the Quinella Trace downriver toward the shade.

He knew what was going to happen before Levi ever got out of the water!

The thought turned her insides cold. And she denied it.

"Oh, my goodness!" She had glided within the shade, unawares.

The cool darkness of massive trees surrounded her. Justice was reminded of what she was supposed to be doing down here at the Quinella. She forced the past away, and the denial, to the back of her mind. Moving on, she watched her feet step silently. Shade and shadow were the only light under full, heavy branches of the huge trees. Weeds were low here and bushes grew lush with moisture but close to the ground. Insects did not shoot up from the ground and whir around her as they would have in sunlight. And here she discovered a multitude of crawling things.

Hearing her own panting breath, Justice clamped her mouth shut. Breathing too hard and fast, she stopped a moment to calm herself. Fear weakened her insides, and she found she was shaking.

Stop too long and you'll never get it done.

Clumsily, she moved up and down the shade close to the trunks of trees. It took her minute upon minute to steady herself. She could hear the sound of an occasional car back on the winding Quinella Road. It took her time until she was brave enough to work her way out, to walk between the trees and the edgewater. There stunted growth gave place to a rocky way, slippery with moss and wild ivy.

Again Justice stood still, this time to watch. She had overheard Thomas tell neighborhood boys how to make a search.

Here I'm about to begin, she thought.

They won't hurt you, Thomas says. Even if one of them attacks, it can't *hurt* you. You are not born being so scared of them, he says. It's what you've heard about them, what you learn wrong about them that makes you so awful terrified.

I am scared. Scared to death, Justice thought. Oh, find one and do what you came to do!

Justice found many. Watching and searching, standing still, soon she was able to separate from green-and-brown shade what looked to be long stripes of grass.

Until they moved.

Thomas beating on his drum—"You don't need to holler like some babies." Telling boys, "Or pick up some sticks and kill."

Striped lengthwise a pale yellow, lying in clumps or beds, all intertwined.

"Bodies are covered with dry scales. You jerks, they ain't slimy to touch. They're 'bout the most useful creatures around. And they always nest at the Quinella Trace. Hundreds of 'em, year after year." Telling boys and drum beating steadily on.

Justice was surrounded by them, bedded in the short grass and in rocky, mossy shelters.

"They can't keep a constant body temperature. So they could die right off if and ever they stayed in hot sun too long."

Justice was horrified by them, but she knew enough to stand still now and to hold her ground. She watched them and waited, which, as Thomas had told, was the best way to fit yourself into their world of quiet and shade. She saw them move, gliding over and under rocks. Some were large, so frightening, maybe three feet long. Others were busy young snakelets whipping around in brand-new skins.

Sweat dripped from her face. A feeling like stripes of cold curled and knotted her stomach. Insects found her feet and crawled over her sneakers.

Stand still as long as there are no spiders. One thing I can't stand is them big brown spiders!

Watching second upon second, she pulled herself in from crawling creatures. She was a small, solid space in a cocoon of time. From its stillness, she saw the garter snakes move by making their skins crawl. Justice became fascinated by the larger snakes. Across their bellies was overlapping skin which seemed to grip the ground and move. Something, maybe muscles inside a snake's body, actually pulled it along.

I wouldn't say they are good-looking creatures, she

thought. They are so awful strange! But sure they aren't ugly as sin, like I'd've sworn they would be.

She saw forked tongues flicker out and in. It was then she forced herself from her safe detachment. She moved ever so carefully.

Just a smallish one for now, she thought. But I'll have to catch the biggest one I can find for The Great Snake Race on Friday.

Snake eyes watched her every move. She stayed two or three feet away from each clump and bed of snakes.

There's only one of me. I'll faint if I think about how many of them!

Her legs felt shaky. She should have eaten breakfast; yet food would have made her sick by now.

I'm weak, I truly am.

She forced herself to head on downriver, searching for youngish snakes. And soon she closed in on a long, skinny garter stretched to its length on a bed of pebbles. At first, she thought it was dead. Then she guessed it had eaten something and was now digesting. Or maybe just resting.

"They eat insects whole," she recalled Thomas saying. And something else, but she'd forgotten some of what he had told.

How could you know what a snake had been up to?

The forked tongue of the snake flickered out and in, lightning fast.

To grab it, move quick but quiet.

The snake slithered, sensing her, perhaps seeing her. It glided over rocks as Justice stood beside it.

Don't let it find a hole.

Well, pick it up.

I can't!

Yes, you *can*—it's what you've come to do. Want the boys to think you're a fool?

But it's so awful hard!

Not when you know it's just a harmless creature. You don't mean to hurt it. And it won't have a mind to hurt you. Go on. Go *on!*

Yeah, that's it.

She knew better than to make a sudden move. She crouched close to the tail of the snake and placed her hands some six inches above it.

The garter commenced moving toward the black-water Trace. Never had Justice seen anything crawl so swiftly. Transfixed by its flow and slither, she nearly let it get away.

Oh, brother!

Her right hand darted sideways and forward. She caught the snake firmly in back of its head, her face screwed up in a terrible grimace as it struggled to free itself. With her left hand, Justice gently took hold of the tail end. And, quaking inside, she was happy to see that her hands were steady. She had done it.

Such a thing—oooh!

Trying not to jerk around, she stood up holding the snake. The garter twisted and slithered in fast motion, trying to get free. Justice held on. Its snake tongue flicked.

Really, just like some miniature lightning in a tiny space. And they aren't slimy, Justice thought.

It felt like a strip of soft leather. Unreasonably, she had expected it to be warm and trembly, sort of like a baby rabbit or hamster. Suddenly, she recalled that snakes were cold-blooded. Sure enough, the garter's skin felt cool.

How to get it in my knapsack on Friday? Not this one, but the big one I have to catch for the Snake Race. She needed a large size for its strength, in case the race was long.

Justice released the snake's head to let it dangle by its tail.

See?

Gazing at it with wonder as it writhed to get loose.

Just take it by the tail and drop it in the sack!

All at once, there was a thin, ugly odor rising from the snake. And Justice let go of it.

"You dirty thing!" It crawled away to disappear at the edge of the river.

That smell—maybe poison! Justice backed away, looking all around her. There were writhing reptiles everywhere underfoot.

Out of here!

And she was running, cutting through the shade as fast as she could without sliding into a snake bed. All she wanted was to get out of the shade into the sun. But the shade didn't end. It went on and on. Finally, she had sense enough to look up at the sky.

Wouldn't you know it?

Those fluffs of white clouds were now low masses with gray undersides.

Never trust *you* again, she thought to the forever sky.

Justice had seen clouds build this way without raining a drop. The sun peeked through them, lighting the tops of trees nearby and then others farther off. It looked like someone had a light and was flashing it on and off through the dark.

There was eeriness about the Quinella Trace lands without strong sunlight. It caused Justice to slow down, think vague, disconnected thoughts as she moved cautiously through the high weeds toward the fence. Where she could, she followed the path she had made coming in. There was a low, hot wind now. It made the weeds swoosh in waves around her knees, as if to engulf her. Fancying snakes and leeches crawling to catch her, Justice nearly screamed.

Nearing the fence, she couldn't find her bike where she had hidden it. Just frantic. And felt like crying.

Someone's stole it!

The idea of her bike getting taken wasn't half so bad as the thought that someone might be watching her.

There it is.

Finding the bike right where she had left it, not four feet from the fence.

"That's what happens when you panic," she told herself.

By the time she and the bike were through the fence again, she was sure it was going to pour down rain on her. The day had grown dreary; it felt full, as though about to burst. Ten minutes later, pedaling and pulling as hard as she could, she had reached the top of the Quinella Road and crossed the silver-smooth tracks of the B&O Railroad.

Justice gave a glance to the tracks as she crossed them:

What'd you go and do—bring this bad weather all the way from Nebraska? Well, we don't want it, either. Better take it back by Friday, too.

She was gone then, hurrying faster than it was safe over Morrey Street, full of potholes. Halfway home, she looked up to find an ugly rain cloud over her head.

It never rained. The day brightened again. Patches of sun broke through and it was hot and still as ever.

Justice turned down the Union Road into her gravel lane and passed under the great old tree.

Cottonwoman! I did it today and I'll be fine on Friday, too.

Still, Justice didn't know how she was supposed to race a

snake. But she didn't intend to let her brothers or any other boys know that.

I'll listen and I'm sure to find out after supper, she thought.

About every other evening, neighborhood boys gathered in the Douglass field; Justice would be sure to be there.

She let her bike fall by the porch steps. There was a sudden thundercrash. Justice grabbed her bike again and hurried with it up onto the porch.

She paused to listen for more thunder, but then smiled grimly. No thunder, it was Thomas. She stood the bike against the porch rail and went to open the front door. As she silently peeked around to her left within the house, a pulse of drumbeating swelled to crash in her face.

Thomas in the living room, seated behind his set of five drums. Still in his pajamas, he was absorbed by the flashing sticks in his hands. He dragged his drum set into the living room each morning. And beat drums from the time he got up until lunchtime, and again after. Later on, he would switch to timpani or kettledrums, as the huge copper drums were most often called. A person had to have a keen sense of pitch and rhythm to play the kettles, Thomas was quick to tell everyone. And he had perfect pitch.

Justice sighed.

What I have to *live* with.

She eased around the door unseen by Thomas and headed for the kitchen in search of Levi. There she found him with the table set. He always made lunch for her and Thomas. Justice had once asked her mother why Levi had to make the sandwiches every day. And her mom had said that Levi never minded, that he liked the responsibility. Justice guessed he did, too, for he never once forgot to make lunch for her. He was at the stove now, concentrating on a skillet too small for the three cheese sandwiches crammed into it.

"Boo," Justice said, coming up behind him. "I left you in the living room."

"Wha—?" Levi whirled around, knocking the skillet across the stove top. He looked stunned, staring at her as if, for a moment, he hadn't known who she was.

"Hey, I was kidding," she said. "You know—I left you *drumming* in the living room. Don't you get it?"

His face had paled. And standing there, speechless, he looked kind of afraid.

"Oh . . . oh, yeah," he said finally. "Ticey. Hi."

"Hi," she said back, wondering at his being so startled.

He laughed nervously and turned back to the stove.

She could tell he hadn't really understood her kidding. Maybe he had just been concentrating too hard on his work. But she felt better when she joked once in a while about her brothers being duplicates of one another. It wasn't fair that she must look in a mirror in order to see herself. All Thomas and Levi had to do was look at one another.

Noise beat steadily from the living room.

"You think he's going to drum like that all summer?" she asked Levi. She was talking to his back and he did not turn around.

"Tice, I have to do this right," he said, and that was all.

At least he hadn't called her Pickle. He hardly ever did when they were alone.

Levi took up a spatula to scrape semi-burned sandwiches from the skillet onto a plate.

"Do you ever want to be like Thomas?" suddenly she thought to ask him.

To be a drummer, she thought. To be so stubborn and willful all the time.

He turned to face her. There was a weary look in his

eyes. It wasn't the first time she had seen it.

"Sometimes I *am* Thomas," he said softly. "I never know when."

She didn't know what to make of that. But she took it as the way one identical might speak offhandedly of the other.

"Does he ever want to be you, you think?" she asked him.

Levi was holding the plate of sandwiches up over the stove, with the spatula on top of them. He had left the skillet smoking, and she reached around him to turn the burner off. She saw his shoulders shudder in rhythm with the beat of Thomas' drums.

"Leave me alone," he said, like a whine. "Just . . . be quiet . . . don't bother me now."

What can you do, she wondered, when your favorite brother says something like that to you?

In some kind of mood, she guessed, and took her seat at the table.

Levi always set the table so nice. There were yellow napkins, white plates and a bowl of potato chips. There was a big bottle of Coke, and ice all ready in the glasses. But she would have enjoyed it much better if her mom had been there making the sandwiches and munching chips as she worked. Levi wasn't one to munch unless he was sitting down eating a meal.

She noticed it was only eleven-thirty. Levi fixed lunch whenever someone was hungry. Must have been Thomas.

If her mom had been here, she would have talked to Justice while she worked. Asking questions. Telling things. Her mom would talk a mile a minute and Justice would, too.

It's so different this summer, Justice thought. Noisy different. It's a weird summer house, she couldn't help thinking, and getting stranger every minute.

"Y'all used to having folks watch over you too close," Justice's friend Mrs. Jefferson liked to say. "Never do, making children too self-conscious. Y'all think you important."

You wouldn't call Levi and Thomas children, would you? Certainly, they weren't to Justice. But wouldn't it be oh so nice if some grown-up would come along and tell Thomas to cut out the racket so much all the time!

Wish Mom were home. In four, five hours she will be.

"Mrs. Leona Bethune Jefferson is better than having nobody," Justice told herself.

Maybe to sneak off and visit her. Justice thought about it.

Biking down the Quinella Road each day, sometimes more than once. She hadn't visited Mrs. Jefferson all week.

If not today, then tomorrow afternoon for sure.

Dimly, she was aware of a peaceful quiet in the house, but then Thomas came charging into the kitchen. Always, he seemed to be bursting with noise. Even his voice exploded from his mouth as though someone had set it off.

Levi was about to serve Justice her sandwich, poised on the greasy spatula.

"D-d-d-ooon't *touch* it, Puh-piii-cle!" Thomas warned her. *"N-n-not* until I-I-hIIII'm *served!"* Drawing out his words and popping them at her.

Oh, brother! she thought. She sometimes thought he stuttered just to annoy her. But she was used to his demanding ways.

Now she and Levi waited patiently as Thomas elaborately seated himself. He smoothed his hair back while peering closely at Levi.

She didn't know how many times she'd seen Thomas

use Levi as his own reflection. Neither of them ever had to use a mirror.

With his fork, Thomas speared a sandwich from the plate before Levi had a chance to serve him one. He drummed his fingers on the table and smoothly told Justice, "Now you may begin."

Grinning like an idiot, she thought to herself.

Thomas wolfed down a third of his sandwich in one huge, disgraceful bite. He eyed Justice with a steady smirk.

There were times when Justice wished he liked her better. But right now she hoped the sandwich would poison him.

Tear him in the gut and flatten him out on the floor.

Until her stomach began to hurt with a deep, cold feeling. Something tore at her insides with slithers of ice. She felt death-weak and knew suddenly that she was about to lose consciousness. But even before she could panic, she had seen a fleeting look of caution come into Thomas' eyes. Quickly, she took up the sandwich and, for strength, hurriedly ate it.

3

It was the hour past suppertime and the neighborhood seemed deserted. The thorny osage hedgerow, twisted by hard weather, spread early-evening shade across half the Douglass field. The trees bordered the length of the west property line; near them, Justice, Thomas and Levi stood in separate pools of dappled sun. Occasionally, there was a wind sigh through the treetops, which made a sound of crowds ohing and ahing from a great distance away. Every now and then, Justice would feel a hot downdraft of air. It caused her tangled, sticky curls to spring up around her ears.

Thomas wore his favorite hat, a purple toque with a large pink ostrich feather stuck in the band. The feather fluttered in princely style, as fragile as a puffball. He appeared feverishly eager, yet confident behind a set of huge copper kettle-drums.

Levi observed his brother, whom he called Tom-Tom, so much a reflection of himself, and his sister, Ticey, trying her best to keep up with the both of them.

Why must she be so excitable? And why couldn't she find girls her age to be friends with? Poor Ticey. It wasn't that she couldn't find any, it was that he and Tom-Tom couldn't keep her away from what they were doing or planning to do. And he supposed it was normal for younger ones to tag after older brothers and sisters.

Levi caught a warm stir of air full in the face. He would have liked to be in the cottonwood tree on the east boundary. He could hear a breeze high up in the brittle osage branches. It might be cooler over in the cottonwood. Yet he remained where he was. Patient and ever alert, he waited for Tom-Tom to tell him, all of them, what was to be.

Behind their field was a high wood fence with a gate in it. The fence separated the field from their backyard. The yard was overgrown on one side with planted beds of flowers—sweet peas, gladioli, hollyhocks, roses—and stubborn, blooming weeds which made that whole side a place wildly beautiful. On the other side of the yard, away from sundown and shade, grew a large, neat vegetable garden. Here Mr. and Mrs. Douglass often spent time when they came home in the afternoon. Hoeing rows of beans, tomatoes and cucumbers was for them a sure way to relax.

Now, after supper, they were on the far side of their white house with black trim, away from the enclosed yard and the open field. Over there was a screened-in porch facing north. It overlooked the front lawn of snowball bushes, evergreen and fruit trees. The Douglasses delighted in sitting on the porch, talking, having tea, after the dishes were washed and put away. And it was not unusual for them to doze a bit there on the porch glider.

Thomas and Levi, with Justice, delighted in the field. In the whole neighborhood, no family had as much open space as they. The acre and a half of field planted years ago in Kentucky bluegrass was kept mowed to an inch of springy turf by Thomas and Levi, taking turns struggling with their rattling gasoline mower. Endlessly, they talked over whose turn it was to mow this time; finally, they divided the field in quarters—one quarter, Thomas; one quarter, Levi—

until the whole field was mowed.

The field had naturally become the sports arena for the neighborhood. It was the football field on one day and the soccer field or gymnasium on the next. Although Thomas and Levi rarely played sports these days, they were quick to supervise and referee all manner of games. This early evening into night, the field would become the gathering place for the Pickle and Cream Gang. The name was a secret of Justice's. She was Pickle. Levi and Thomas were the cream of the crop, better than other boys.

The field looked vast and empty in the growing shade as the three of them faced it, their backs toward the fence.

Thomas squinted down the field at backyards, some with low hedges, whose houses fronted on the wide Dayton Street. He clutched four felt-tipped kettledrum sticks, two in each hand. Momentarily, his face seemed trapped behind the sticks as he turned his purple toque hat this way and that. He peered at Levi, his mirror, searching for the proper angle for the hat. When he had the slant at which the tall feather caught the best of any moving air, he lowered his hands. And struck the calfskin drumheads with the sticks in a low, trembling sound.

The tone was so deep and sudden it startled Justice. She moved closer to Levi. But he, in turn, stepped aside and somewhat away from both Thomas and Justice. She was left alone, glancing anxiously from one brother to the other. Thomas' kettledrums were the "instruments of torture" for her, more so than his regular set of snares and bass drum. They were like witches' boiling cauldrons from which powerful sound bubbled and overflowed.

In just a few minutes, Justice would be the only girl and the only eleven-year-old in the entire field. Thomas wouldn't allow other girls around—not to say that they were much interested. And he tolerated Justice because his folks made him.

Sound from one kettledrum began to build into a bass roar that rolled down the field and on through the hedges to hit houses. He could almost see that sound bounce away and sail over front lawns to escape into Dayton Street. He kept up the unholy racket until Mr. Buford Jefferson came out of his back door to see what was the commotion. Mr. Jefferson must have been on his way out, in any case. For he carried his black lunchbox and wore his green-and-orange baseball cap pulled low over his eyes. Jefferson was night watchman at the GE plant about eighteen miles up the highway. He was also one of the Little League coaches with an awful sour disposition. Maybe because his son, Dorian, refused to play baseball. Right now was about time for Mr. Jefferson's team practice before he went off to work.

"Hey, Lee," Thomas yelled across to Levi. The overwhelming drum roll he made would keep anyone down the field from hearing him clearly. Levi couldn't hear him, either. "He didn't have to come out the back like that," Thomas yelled.

"What?" Levi shouted back.

"Jefferson!" Thomas hollered. "He could've gone out the front to his car—I said, HE DIDN'T HAVE TO COME OUT THE BACK."

"Oh," Levi said. He didn't feel up to yelling above the kettledrumming. Since the beginning of the summer when Tom-Tom borrowed the drums, he had grown gradually accustomed to their powerful strength of sound. But if they went on too long, he would feel light-headed and forget what he was doing.

48

"Jefferson wants to let me know he'd like to kill me!" Thomas yelled.

"Maybe he's just curious," Levi was forced to yell back. The drums rolling and vibrating on air were deafening.

"Yeah, sure!" Thomas yelled.

Justice realized that shouting at the top of his lungs was something Thomas did with little effort. And Levi was just starting to feel dizzy when Thomas changed the drumming to a foreboding pom-pom on one kettle, to a pom-pom-uh on the other, pitched to a fifth tone of the first. He alternated this pounding on the drumheads; he swayed from side to side. The ostrich feather jumped and leaped as though charged with electricity.

"Look at that old fogey staring!" Thomas shouted. "Sure glad Dad ain't fifty years old!"

Their dad was forty-one, which was old enough. But Mr. Buford Jefferson was fifty going on a century, Thomas was sure of it. And mean to his kid, Dorian. And at times mean to his wife, Mrs. Leona Jefferson. To Thomas, she looked to be at least one hundred and sixty-seven years ancient, and *really* strange.

"You'll be an old man one day!" Levi thought to yell back.

"Aw, you read too many books!" Thomas shouted.

Mr. Jefferson stared up the field. The outline of him was coiled in a fierce resistance to the noise. Abruptly, he sprang to his right. Defiantly, he disappeared around his house. Right after he had turned the corner, they heard the sound of a motor starting up.

It was then their gate swung open and their dad stepped through into the field.

Mr. Douglass was not a tall man, but he had an assurance about him that was commanding. Justice had his exact build and she would be lucky if she grew to average height for a woman. Mr. Douglass' brown skin was tanned a deeper hue, caused by working out-of-doors as he did a good part of the time. His people had been stone-carvers, and he himself was one of the best stonecutters in the area. He was always in demand, even when construction work was slow. And he could size fieldstone into any shape for a fireplace or chimney. With a. steel mallet and a chisel, he would break a heavy stone in half. He'd chip away at half of the stone until he had the jagged shape he needed. Whatever the shape, it would fit perfectly.

Mr. Douglass glanced from Justice to Levi, then steadied his gaze on Thomas. A slight irritation, a bristling seemed to come over him.

"People don't want that kind of noise," he told Thomas. "Stop it now, and bring those drums inside."

Thomas seemed to pale, then turned dark with anger. Hands still drumming, he said through his teeth, "It's not *noise!* It's . . ." Suddenly, he ceased drumming. Levi had caught his eye, and his voice trailed off.

Lee knew it would never do for Tom-Tom to start in arguing with their dad. Not if he meant to put on a show with the drums this evening. Lee could tell by his brother's expression that Tom-Tom had been thinking about taking a stand.

So Levi walked over to his dad and stood before him with that way of planting his feet together as they do in the military. He had his father's full attention. Standing still, respectful, he captured his dad's interest.

Justice listened as Levi explained how Thomas felt he was ready to play kettledrums for all of the kids. Tom-Tom had learned some new things about drumming this summer, Levi said. The kids were always coming over to the house throughout the day, bothering Tom-Tom to teach them. Boys were just so fascinated with the way the big drums worked, he explained. Sure, neighbors heard, but they didn't get angry. They understood, Levi said, that Tom-Tom was truly a drummer. And now the boys would be coming to the field and Tom-Tom would teach them.

Maybe boys did come to the house, Justice thought. But if they did, she hadn't seen them. Most boys were a little shy of coming right up to the front door, and, particularly, of Thomas. It was easier for them to come into the field. Levi had lied smoothly. She suspected all of it was a lie. Not like Levi at all.

"Well. You see he keeps it down most of the time," Mr. Douglass was saying.

"I will," Levi said.

"And see he doesn't go on too long."

Levi nodded. He felt dizzy and slightly headachy. He was having trouble recalling what he and his dad had been saying only a moment ago.

Justice was happy that the fun would continue. She skipped over to her dad, grinning from ear to ear.

Mr. Douglass caught her around the neck, eyes softening as he looked down at her. "Why don't you come on over to the porch?" he said to her. "Tell us about what you did today?"

Laughing, thankful for his asking. "Maybe in a little while," she said, and then: "Can I have a tomato from the garden?"

"In a little while," he said, joking. "Ticey, curly-top," he added, brushing his hand through her tangled ringlets.

She knew she was her dad's favorite. She could tell by the way he was always so kind to her. He had a joke for her each and every day, and he let her have her way.

Levi knew their dad protected Ticey because she was small. And because not only did she have two older brothers, but brothers who were identicals. He wondered what it was like for her to be a singleton. And it eased his mind somehow, knowing his dad would be there each night for Ticey.

To put things straight, he thought. To make it all come out even.

After her dad had left the field, Justice turned around and around in terrific circles until the earth spun in a rush of flowing color and she fell to the ground in a crumpled heap of laughter. She lay giggling, with a sensation of wind rushing in her ears. By the time she was on her feet again, Thomas was staring her down with the purest, meanest expression she had ever seen. While her dad had been there, she had forgotten about Thomas. He had a way of making himself unnoticed when he needed to.

I'm awful glad you can still drum, she thought of telling him. But then she thought better of it. No need to cause him to say something mean. I won't be silly again, she thought, her earnest face pleading with him.

Whyn't you just disappear? his eyes seemed to say.

For protection, Justice hurried to the fence, where Levi was standing.

Right then, Dorian Jefferson came sprinting around the left side of his house into his backyard. He came to a halt at the back hedge, back-pedaled to his porch and made a solid forward run for the hedge again.

He made a perfect leap over, Levi observed. But he fell,

skidding on his hip for ten feet into the grassy field. He rolled over on his stomach and pounded the earth in a silent tantrum. Thomas let go a mighty roar of the drums —too late for the action—and they all had to laugh.

Dorian could be the most comical boy, Justice knew, with jiggles of energy that caused his arms and legs to never stop moving. As Thomas' drums rolled smoothly on, she pulled herself up as straight and tall as possible, the way Levi was standing.

They watched Dorian leap, zag and cartwheel his way up the field. Thomas was quick to match the bounding movement on his drums. And the whole land—trees, sky and field—boomed and crashed, shaking the birds out of branches. Blackbirds sprang up to the high, hot air and, wheeling, winged their way west to open country.

Other boys began to appear now, as if by signal. They came off the street, through backyards and around property lines into the Douglass field. Some ran all of the way. And these Thomas greeted with a rush of rolling beats that seemed to come in waves. A few boys took their time coming in, trying to ignore the hypnotic roar of the kettles. Thomas matched the lazy, halting rhythm of their strides. With arms folded, two boys made a show of whispering and laughing loudly. Pretending that Thomas, his drums, so out of place in the field, and even Justice and Levi were the worst kind of showoffs.

Thomas gave them a few snide beats: DA-RUM, DA-RUM! POM PA-RA POM-POM (OH, WHAT A FEELING!)

These two boys were the last to find their way into the shade, where they faced stares and snickers from the rest of the boys already seated in a semicircle around Thomas' copper kettles.

53

Thomas tipped back a foot pedal, lowering the pitch of one drum. He toned both drums down to the sound of waves washing ashore, perhaps heard through closed windows.

"You guys wanna come play, you come on time!" he yelled at them. "Don't be coming like you got something better to do—'cause you know you *ain't*. Not unless you wanna do something like hittin' a dumb ball with a foolish stick a *wood*."

Boys who had come on time watched and listened in awe. The two who had come over in spite of themselves grinned uneasily and hung their heads.

Levi gave a quick glance to Dorian Jefferson. The boy rested in a sprint-start position on one leg. He was dirty, as usual, and ragged, not because he had to be, but because nobody in his house took notice of or seemed to care how he looked. Levi knew that Tom-Tom's snide remark about "dumb" baseball had been directed at Dorian's father. He hoped Tom-Tom wouldn't insult any of the boys. For he never liked confronting his brother—how easy it was to substitute this vague thought for the truth!—and he hated the rare times when they quarreled.

For the moment, Levi was content to lean comfortably against the fence. He thought how easily Tom-Tom could bring a pack of boys together and control them. Levi never wanted or needed to do that. Yet, watching his brother, he was struck once again by the familiar notion that he watched himself.

The drums beat steadily. Thomas gazed around the field. He focused on Justice at the fence near Levi and gave her a searing look of menace. He stared at her for a full ten seconds, ceasing to drum and holding the sticks poised above the drumheads. His pink plume stood straight up, trembling.

Every boy followed Thomas' gaze. They all looked at Justice, smirking at her until she crumbled inside. Feeling miserable and short, she slunk away as Levi unfolded his arms.

It was then she heard him say softly: "Don't go. Stand by the gate."

She stood at the gate, pretending she would fix something on the latch.

"How come she has to be here?" she heard one boy say.

Levi waited, guessing that Tom-Tom struggled with feelings of spite toward Justice, of family loyalty, and an urge to put the boy down.

"*You!*" Thomas ground out the word. "Youuu . . . youuuu—" Hanging it there like a question; and on the same note: "—got-a rrright-to-say-wh-who . . . who caaan come-into-this-field?" Almost singing at the boy. "*Iiii* say-who-can-be . . . be-*here!*" he said, still in a single, but lower tone. He added, "Me-and . . . Lee . . . *both.*" Bursting through his teeth.

"Mom and Dad say Justice can be here." Levi spoke reasonably. "Or else nobody can play here."

Thomas began a drum roll, drowning out Levi. But they all had heard him.

Justice hung on the gate, peeking at them under her arm. She was glad to be at a distance where the boys and Thomas would most likely come to ignore her. She could still watch them and hide herself behind Levi as well.

"Now," Thomas said, with a flourish of flailing arms. The sticks beat the drums with tremendous force.

All at once, he stopped. One of the boys was saying,

"Ough, ooh, it's too loud—save me!"

They all could see Thomas go tense. But then he relaxed and beat the drums with moderation, in jazz figures, repeating them again and again. There were riffs of complex beats and rhythms. And they varied in depth from somewhat loud to a pulsation more felt than heard.

Through a blur of sticks, they saw Thomas flicking hand screws without missing a beat. They listened as the tone rose and fell from the shimmering copper kettles and rose again. Thomas leaned slightly over one drum, his tall plume flicking and leaping.

What had first struck them as jumbled blasts of noise, they soon distinguished as thrilling sound. Soon no one needed to tell the boys they were privileged to hear a masterful drummer. They watched and listened with rapt attention as the drums beat on and on.

Levi's fingers began to twitch of their own accord. He was having a sudden, urgent sensation of what it must be like to hold the felt sticks and make such wonderful sound.

Thomas' talent had been discovered by someone whose job it was to notice. His teacher, Mr. Phil Grier, had brought the kettledrums over as soon as school was out so Thomas could use them all summer long. They belonged to Mr. Grier personally and not to the school. And everyone had been impressed that he would lend Thomas such valuable equipment.

Levi had no apparent talent, although he enjoyed writing prose as well as poetry. He wrote easily, constantly, telling no one. He felt no envy for Tom-Tom and the crowds of kids he attracted. Summers could be the worst times. For, with little to do, Thomas had in the past gotten into trouble with their dad. Usually, he had dragged Levi in with him.

So Levi was glad that Tom-Tom could do something so special. Also, this way, Tom-Tom's attention focused elsewhere than on Levi.

Thomas did poorly in school, almost as if he tried. Rude to teachers, contemptuous, he made poor marks in conduct. He was smart enough, Levi knew. But he would have flunked his subjects if not for Levi's steady coaching at home.

Through the roll and echo of deep drumming, Justice discovered the twitching of Levi's hands. He was perspiring, glistening with sweat, although the shade had cooled the field somewhat. It was a mystery to her why Levi's hands had to twitch. No other boy's hands did that.

Thomas beats the drums and Levi's hands make to do the same. So who's the copy-cat?

Justice couldn't believe that Levi would want to be a drummer. Oh, she'd heard Thomas drumming for her whole life, it seemed like. And just because he'd thought to bring those big, sickening drums outdoors, everybody had to go make him something special. See the way they look at him! Before, Thomas hadn't brought anything bigger than a parade drum outside.

Standing there with that dumb, moth-eaten hat, she thought. Like it makes him some better than Levi. Because he got it from them Ultramunda actors the last time the straggly troupe came to town. With their circus tent and their made-up faces!

Anybody can wear a hat. And play drums, too.

She was sure of this, if and when the drums were that terrible loud. Even a monkey wouldn't have any trouble playing them.

Suddenly, Thomas made the drums sound comical. Fleetingly, Justice wondered how it was possible he could do that.

Sitting utterly still, the boys sensed the change in the air. They screwed up their faces, covered their ears at the crashing shenanigans. Some jumped up, knocking into one another. Others staggered around and fell down again. Suddenly, boys were wiggling and crawling on their stomachs like the worst unbearable pain had hit them. Moaning and groaning, they were putting on quite a rambunctious show themselves.

They made Justice about sick to death. But, in spite of that, she would have loved to be as free to play around in the field as they were. Why couldn't she? Yet she knew the answer to that. It made her sad to be so alone and left out of things.

Through the din, Levi had to smile. He caught Tom-Tom's eye, and identical smug grins flowed between them.

The comical drumming had been a lead-in, something Levi had recognized the moment the boys began slithering on the ground. The thunderous sound of kettledrums ceased abruptly, as somehow he'd known they would. Such an immense, sudden absence of noise froze the boys in twisted poses.

"*Youuuu* snakes-in-the-grass!" Thomas screeched at them.

Shocked, they sat up, looking like a bunch of babies wakened from sleep. Then, again alert, they settled into their semicircle. All eyes watched Tom-Tom.

The drums rolled softly. "Well, I ain't no snake-charmer," he told them. "I'm the Major Drummer and I lead the parade. Except we ain't going on any march.

"And you guys won't be some little snakes in the grass," he said.

The drums sounded deeply, but as if from a great distance: "The Great Snake Race is my snake race . . . ," Thomas chanted.

A staccato beat began on one drum: "Is my great race. . . ." On the other drum, a long, resounding roll: "Is a race for snakes. . . ."

Both drums rolling. Smooth, like the sound of rivers: "The Great Snake Race won't be just snatching snakes.

"Y'all have to hold them." (Boom-pah!)

"You got to sack 'em and keep 'em in." (Pom-pa-pom/ POM-PA-POM!)

" 'Cause snakes can get out-a most anything." (A-ret-te-tet-tee!)

"They can get out-a *hand.*" (A-rolica-rolica/Pom-pa-POM-POM!)

Justice watched Levi. With eyes shining at his brother, he wore a strange grin. It was Thomas' smirk stretched across his face.

A long drum roll echoed through the trees and sundown. They all did glance to westward, where the osage trees of the Douglass property twisted black and were back-lighted by a spectacular red sun going down. It didn't look real to them, that blood-red sun, and it didn't look painted. It looked as if it would burn down the horizon. It would sear out a trench and come sliding all the way back to them.

Sure, Justice thought. Red sun at night is a sailor's delight.

They none of them knew much about sailors. But she guessed that the rhyme she'd heard somewhere would hold true for The Great Snake Race. It meant that tomorrow would bring another day of hot, cloudless weather. And if Thursday was going to be fine, then Friday had a good chance of being the same.

Drums sounded a steady but soft pom-pom/pom-pom.

"Any you guys ever catch some snakes?" Thomas said, his voice pitched just loud enough to be heard.

Boys looked at one another. They were uncertain whether to say anything, for fear Tom-Tom would produce a snake and make them snatch it.

A boy spoke timidly. "I did, once."

"I buried one once," said a kid named Slick Peru. "But I didn't catch it. It were already dead."

Boys snickered.

"I caught a water moccasin once," Talley Williams said. Sitting in front, he was a plump, friendly boy and had come on time.

"No, you didn't," Tom-Tom told him through the pom-pom beat. "You might think you caught one. But nobody in they right mind go catching water moccasins."

"Because they venoms," Dorian Jefferson said.

" 'Cause they're venomous," Tom-Tom corrected him. "Poisonous," he added. "And if you see anything out there Friday that don't look like a garter snake"—Pom/pom/pom—"you walk away from it."

You mean, there are *poisonous* snakes out there? Justice thought.

"I'll kill anything that's not a garter," Dorian said. "I'll grind 'em in the ground!"

"No, you won't!" Tom-Tom yelled at him. The drumming ceased. "An-an-anybody st-starting in-killling . . . snakes-for-sp . . . sp . . . sport-is . . ."

". . . disqualified," Levi finished for him.

"Yeah, annn-dh c-c-caaan't never be . . ."

". . . in The Great Snake Race," Levi finished again.

"I *thought* it was a water moccasin," Talley Williams said. "It was whipping through the water."

Water moccasins! And I fooled around out there! Justice thought.

Thomas' sticks made a blur as a delicate rolling sound began.

"That's another thing," he said easily. "You don't catch nothing is in the water. Stay out of the water. The Quinella Trace has a mess a leeches in it."

Thomas stared pointedly at Levi. Pom-ah/pom-ah sounding from the drums in a whisper.

Justice felt a chill crawl over her. It hurt her so deep inside to see Levi hang his head.

"I told you about the leeches before," Thomas was saying to the boys.

"My dad says there ain't a leech in that water," Dorian said.

"Sure, your dad knows a lot," Thomas said. "I mean"— Pom/pom/pom—"between yelling his head off at the Little League"—laughter from the boys—"and throwing a fit 'cause the car won't start"—Pum-pa-pom—"when does he have any time for fishing at the Quinella—huh?"

Boys whooped, "Ooh, cold on Dorian!"

"He say he going move on out of here, too—my daddy," Dorian said when they had quieted. He turned away from them.

"Going to move what from where?" Tom-Tom said, brimming with impatience. Only his hands moved.

"Going to move Mom and me and him. And pretty soon, too," Dorian said. "Say he don't like the feeling of this place."

"He just talking," Slick Peru said. But he glanced uncertainly at Tom-Tom.

"Y'all be here forever," another told him.

Tears welled in Dorian's eyes. They were tears of anger and gratitude, tears which Levi saw him blink away.

"My daddy says . . . ," Dorian went on unsteadily, ". . . says can't even Jesus save all you Douglasses." He wrapped his arms around to cover his head.

"Why he has to pick on us all the time!" Thomas said, to no one in particular. He did give a glance at Levi, and Levi gave him back a look of warning to take it easy.

"My daddy says this field oughtn't be y'all's," Dorian said. "Says to make it a baseball diamond for everybody, too."

"Sure, so he won't have to spend a nickel for gas getting over to his Little League," Thomas couldn't help saying. But he left off. His drums ceased. He was silent a moment, staring at the boy.

He's lying. He's making the whole thing up, Justice thought vaguely about Dorian, she didn't know why. Dorian never had lunch money, was the next thing she thought about. In school, kids gave him nickels and dimes, or they gave him part of their own lunches. When the Jeffersons first arrived last year, this happened about once a month. By the end of this year, it was happening most every day and kids resented it. It wasn't as if his parents couldn't afford to buy his lunch. It was as though his mom, especially, wanted him to hustle it from the kids.

"Dorian," Thomas said, drumming the instant he spoke the name. "Just don't mention to your dad about the race for snakes, hear? And don't any the rest of you say anything about it, either."

"Man, maybe Dorian shouldn't even be in on it, too," Talley Williams said.

62

Dorian leaped to his feet in a second in an exaggerated fighting stance.

"Don't get yourself all upset," Thomas told him. He played a soothing beat until Dorian had settled down again. "He gets to be in it like everybody else," Thomas told Talley. "But get out a line and you are out, Dorian, understand? That goes for the rest of you guys, too.

"Now." Thomas looked them over and then all around. His drums seemed to pause.

Shade covered the entire field. Dogs could be heard barking for nothing, announcing their progress through town. Cars were sounding along Dayton Street. Over in the park, the Little League practice must have been coming to an end. There was a suspended stillness from that far away, punctuated every once in a while with a yell. The high wind had breezed itself out and the line of ancient osage orange trees was still.

Boys leaned forward toward Thomas. Justice had worked her way up to a point next to him and slightly behind. No boy paid any attention to her.

"C-c-caaatching snakes-won't-be . . . nuh-nuh-near theee whole-thing youuu got-to-do on Fr-frriday," Thomas told them. The sticks he'd been holding still began a beat and he spoke smoothly. "You got to sack them and bike 'em back here."

Wide-eyed, the boys turned and stared at one another.

"We get them back here and string 'em in the trees." He pointed to the twisted osage. "Until Saturday and the countdown."

"Whaaa?" Boys began to holler. "You going to make us hang snakes in the trees?"

Thomas spoke carefully with the drums rolling softly. "I *said*, we going to hang the *sacks* of snakes in the trees. Back

63

in there where the leaves are thickest, in on the low branches where no one will notice. See, the branches grow across-ways, looking for sunlight. If you can't listen no better than that, y'all ought to quit now while you ahead."

"The *sacks* of them!"

"I thought he mean—"

"Try not to think," Thomas scolded them. "Leave the thinking to the Major Drummer!"

He let the kettles roar. Sound hit the boys like a sudden front of thunderous weather.

"Yeoow!" Boys fell back as if wind had knocked them over.

"Okay, you guys," Thomas said, silencing the drums. He stood at attention before the boys until they had again settled back. The drums commenced to hum seemingly of their own accord.

"See," he told them, "snakes can get loose of most anything, except a sack you can draw real tight-closed at the top. But that kind of draw-sack—you know, like you keep trunks and towels in for the town pool—that kind of sack has to be made of stuff that'll let the snakes breathe free air through. Easier for you is to have one of the big plastic peanut-butter containers. With the handles and the lids." He studied each one of the boys to make certain they understood.

"You punch little holes in the lids," he told them, "and hang the containers up by the handles. See if you got any. Most folks have 'em."

He waited a moment before continuing; but the humming drums did not cease. "It's just for one night," he told them. "Part of The Great Snake Race, of which I am the sole inventor, is to find out if you guys can keep them snakes overnight and keep a secret, too. Because you have to have the snakes on Saturday. *Alive.* And no mom or dad to know, either.

"No wounded snakes and no dead snakes count for The Great Snake Race on Saturday," Thomas finished finally.

"But I thought—" Justice spoke before she realized. She'd been listening closely to Thomas. Now Levi gave her a look to shush her.

She whispered to him, "I thought it was going to be just on Friday."

"Friday and Saturday. You're not supposed to talk," he whispered back.

It annoyed her that he, too, followed along, giving Thomas the right to say who could talk and when.

Next thing, he'll be telling us when to breathe.

But she stayed quiet, for The Great Snake Race began to loom large, like the small patch of gray on a horizon that built into a summer storm.

Two days! she thought. Keep the snakes caged and keep them alive! I bet the biggest is the best for staying curled up in a sack. And best for racing.

She didn't dare think what it would be like to catch and handle a large snake. Even the skinny snake she'd handled had had strength which surprised her.

Get it in a sack fast as you can and bring it on home.

There was quiet. Stillness rushed them in the absence of drumming. Thomas spoke eagerly: "Fr-frriday, tuh-ten o'clock. Weee meet-at thee Quin-*ella* Trace." Words popping and bursting. "You-you youuuu got-as muh-muuch *time* as you-you neeed *tooo* catch 'em, but . . . buuuut *don't* tuh-tuh-tuh-ake forever!"

"Better make a limit," Levi told him; then, quietly, in the

same voice as Thomas': "You've forgotten to drum."

"O-oh," Thomas said, in Levi's voice.

His hands moved, not with any kind of speed that Justice could see. All the same, the drumsticks became a blur. And sound, like a mystery in a minor key, rose and fell and echoed all around them.

"Two hours is the limit of time to hunt the snakes," Thomas said easily. "Then bring 'em back and string 'em up." Softly, the drums rolled. "You can leave 'em over there in the trees until Saturday morning, early."

"How early?" someone asked him.

"While your folks still be sleeping," he said. "Six-thirty."

"Aw, Tom-Tom, too early, man," said Slick. "Saturday, my mom is asleep even by nine-thirty."

"Then you got it made," Thomas told him.

"Yeah, but then *I* can't sleep late," Slick said.

"My dad sleeps all day," Dorian said eagerly. He looked happy, all thought of tears gone now. "But my mom's around. Don't know what-all time she starts up." They knew his mom wouldn't pay any attention to his going.

Wonder how she's feeling, thought Justice.

Other boys were moaning, "Why so early?"

Thomas gave them a blast of the kettles. He flicked hand screws, changing tones to unearthly, magnificent sound.

The boys quieted. Without their having noticed, a thin mist had gathered over the field. It rose from the ground like shadow.

"Y'all have to be such babies!" Thomas said. "You be up here by six-thirty and you come *quiet!*"

What Tom-Tom hadn't told them, but what Levi knew, was that they dare not wake their own parents on Saturday. They mustn't let them know about the snake race. Levi was certain that his mom, especially, wouldn't take kindly to pails and sacks of snakes hanging in the trees.

"He'll do it every time," he said to himself about Tom-Tom. Hope nothing goes wrong.

Drumming, Thomas told them: "You have all day tomorrow to find some of them plastic pails. Don't anybody come in here on Friday without one or a good drawsack."

"We got this yellow *big* pail with a handle at home," Dorian said. "Only, it's about halfway full of peanut butter."

The boys laughed at him.

"Empty," Thomas said. "Halfway *empty* of peanut butter." He beat one drum absently.

"Yeah," Dorian said, "I can scoop up the peanut butter and make it in a ball with two hands. And . . . and hide it in the freezer!"

"Don't fool around!" Thomas told him, with the boys snickering.

"I'm not fooling," Dorian said.

Why is he acting stupid? Justice wondered.

"Dorian," Thomas said, "you do something dumb, like hiding peanut-butter balls, and your mom or dad'll find out what we're doing for sure."

"Oh. Well," Dorian said, "I'll eat it all up tonight."

"Man—Dorian, you just come on Friday. I'll have a pail for you." Thomas gave a glance to Levi to see if this would be all right.

Levi didn't make a move that Justice could see. But with his eyes he gave agreement to Thomas. She knew that if one of her brothers was to fix up a pail for Dorian, it wouldn't be Thomas. Thomas never fixed up anything, or took care of anything, except his drums. Levi even made Thomas' bed and cleaned up their room. And that made Justice mad.

There wasn't a soul to help her out with keeping her room straight.

Expect me to pick up everything myself, she thought. And make the bed . . . hang up all my clothes . . .

Not many months ago, her mom had made her bed each morning, and picked up the mess of her room. Justice had had clean, ironed clothes every day. Now all had changed. She suspected that nothing would ever be the same.

I don't like it here, she thought. Why don't I go around to sit awhile with Mom and Dad?

She knew why. She never could pull herself away when the boys were gathered. She could not help herself, for, like a moth, she was captured by their light.

A POM sounded on one kettledrum and a Pom again on the other, a third tone higher than the first. The beat swelled in drum rolls huge and deep. So massive a sound surrounded them that Justice believed it must have lifted Levi to his feet, as it had some of the other boys. It was a sound of such strength it had to have brought the twilight. While she could see Levi, the features of his face seemed to have run together. Just as if a cloth had wiped away his eyes, nose and mouth. Glad she was that sunlight had vanished. Tomorrow would come that much sooner, and so, on to Friday.

Justice looked around the field at the boys, who were also featureless. She saw again the great cottonwood tree on the east boundary.

Cottonwoman, so silent.

She'd caught hold of the darkening and was arranging it around her.

Thomas was a shadow hunched over two dark pools. Sound rolled and resounded from the kettles. It floated the boys by twos down the field, through a wispy film of mist. The boys drifted away.

Wait!

They had no bodies.

How do you race the snakes?

Justice could pick out heads of boys like bobbing balloons. But she couldn't tell which head was which.

The field emptied, except for the three of them. Musky odor of perspiration mixed with the scent of grass on the heat of night. Wordlessly, her brothers prepared to leave. They pulled a dolly from beneath an osage. The low truck was homemade, with wheels they had scrounged. They picked up drop-cloths to cover the kettle drums. Then they placed the drums on the dolly.

She held the gate wide open for them as they strained to handle the dolly through. And surprised she was to see porch lights on at the house. Justice thought how sweet the lights looked, of safety, as her brothers struggled up the backyard.

She took a last look at the field. Nothing much to see but night coming quickly on. A field of grass darkening. When she was older, she would take a turn mowing it—she would make them let her. Osage trees were one mass. Houses down there—Dorian's, the Stevenson place next to his—were all of them lighted. She felt warm. The night had stayed hot.

When is it gonna cool?

She had a jumble of thoughts. Who would've thought the Pickle and Cream Gang was here minutes ago?

And drums. And rolling noise.

Loved it, too. Every minute. Hope it happens again.

Good night, everybody, she thought to houses down the field.

'Night, Cottonwoman, see you tomorrow.

Justice waited, but there was no real answer from the cottonwood tree.

Already asleep, Justice thought. Vaguely, she wondered if the cottonwoman had heard her.

Anyone can race a snake. Nothing to it.

Pulling the gate closed, she reached the house in two leaps, it felt like, of her churning legs.

Before darkness could trip her up and right after Thomas had closed the door in her face.

4

She had a jump-rope and had wound it around her wrists to shorten it. Already, she had jumped hundreds of times without missing, and she was still jumping.

She was singing, " 'One-day. Stew-day. A bake-day, coming up,' " but her lips didn't move.

In the field, the osage trees bowed down, waving at her with the slow motion of plants under water.

" 'Four-day. Boil-day. Here's a Fry-day.' "

It was night in the field. She could see as though it were day. Midday sun warmed her back, although there was no sun shining. The sun-night didn't seem odd to her.

Jumping rope made a noise—whum-uhk—each time the rope turned through the air and hit the ground. She jumped in an old pair of boots belonging to Thomas. They were too big and floppy, and half full of rainwater. Her socks were soaked through, but she didn't mind. Everything around her, the whole field, was black and shiny with rain.

Must've poured real hard.

The field became a glistening river. Justice stopped the rope to get a better look at it. But she couldn't stop jumping. With each jump, she came closer to the river water.

Don't fall in!

She curled her toes, screaming, and made no sound. She

held her breath to keep from jumping. Yet, in no time she was at the edge of the black river.

The rope shivered in her hands. Cool and leathery, it wiggled and slithered. She let go of it and it dropped into her boot. Tightening around her ankle, the rope bit her toes.

Justice fell into the river on her stomach. She held her breath until the need for air forced her to breathe water. Black water filled her nostrils and her mouth. She gulped it down eagerly, hoping to drink up the river before she had to become a fish.

Something pounded and pounded as she woke up. Gasping for air, Justice sat straight up and nearly screamed out of fear. Slowly, she came to recognize her room. She was in bed, where she was supposed to be. The pounding was her own heart racing.

The dream vanished completely in her warm, dry room, with the earliest morning light pressed against the windows.

My nose is stuffed up. Maybe why I couldn't breathe.

She had kicked her covers into a ball at the foot of the bed. Her pillow was on the floor.

I'm never going to sleep again.

Frightened, she would've liked to call for her mom.

Must be still very early.

Instead of calling out, she managed to straighten the sheet and blanket and pull them over her. Leaning out over the edge of the bed, she snatched her pillow from the floor as if plucking a babe from water. And curled herself into a ball with the covers and pillow over her head.

Now I'm safe.

She was safest of all when no part of her—head, toes or elbows—was left uncovered. But after a minute there wasn't enough air to breathe. Smothering, she punched a small hole leading out from under the pillow. A nice stream of air made its way to her. She took deep breaths until she felt calm; still, she kept her eyes wide open.

I'll wait for Mom or Dad to get up. Dad first, I guess. Has to be still early enough for him. I won't sleep again.

Somewhere within the staring into the safety of her bedclothes, she did fall asleep again. It was a fitful sleep with no clear dreams. A nothingness, with sudden bursts of meaningless words. She recognized the sound of them as the single voice of herself, Thomas and Levi.

"Us. Three," the voice said.

Justice was afraid.

Later, she awoke with a start to the tinny, chim/chi-chim/, chim/chi-chim/ of Thomas' standing cymbals. She had slept long enough to erase the memory of the last dream. And she lay awhile, listening to the steamy rhythms from the living room. Justice could appreciate cymbals more than she could drums. They made a restful sound, somehow mixed yellow and dusty with bright sunlight now streaming into her room.

Suddenly, Thomas added the quiet-shattering boom of the bass drum. From then on, the noise of drums and crashing cymbals was ear-splitting. She knew she had to get up and out of the house. She rolled out, pulling clean things from her bureau. She dressed in a flash in a T-shirt and a last clean pair of jeans, and avoided looking at a mess of pajamas, belts, games and books in a jumble on the floor. Racing to the bathroom, she washed her face and neck and managed to comb about half of her hair before she gave up. There were tangles like rats' nests, and these she cut out with a pair of dull scissors she found in the cabinet. She sat up on the sink with her face a couple of inches from the mirror, and snipped and sawed away. Justice cut until she was satisfied that nothing she could do would make her hair look any better. Then she climbed back down, cleaning the sink of every trace of hair.

There was no way for her to reach the kitchen from the bathroom hall without going through the living room. She would have avoided Thomas if she could have, but there was no way.

Hope breakfast isn't all dried out.

She thought of her mom, who knew how all alone she felt the first thing in the day and would have made breakfast for her before going off to work.

Why'd I have to sleep so late? Now I won't see her until way this afternoon.

Maybe Levi is having his breakfast, she thought. No, he'll be through. Thomas won't eat anything before eleven. And then go right ahead and eat a big lunch. Enough to make a normal person sick to her stomach!

Rushing into the parlor at full speed, she began shouting her lungs out in the hope of startling the drummer.

"Thomas, will you cut it out? It's awful! I hate it!"

She could have been a gray wall with a dull landscape hanging from it for all of the interest Thomas showed her. His head continued to bob and weave as he patted the cymbals and the snare with his brushes, with a boom from the bass drum in rhythm.

"You just can't *do* this every day like you're the only person here," Justice told him. "It's not normal—*we* live here, too!"

It registered on her that Levi lay stretched out on the couch. His head was veiled in a thin cloud of smoke. He pressed two fingers on the bridge of his nose—eyes closed—while one foot tapped in time with Thomas' drumming. In the other hand he held a lighted cigarette.

Levi must have heard Justice, but he made no notice. He took a deep draw from the cigarette and breathed it out. Then he lifted his arm straight up and back over his shoulder. Thomas, sitting somewhat behind the couch, leaned forward over his drums and took a draw from the cigarette. He never missed a beat.

"You *guys!*" Justice couldn't believe her eyes. "What are you *doing?* You're smoking—is that grass? Wait until I tell Mom!"

Both of them gazed at her without comment. She felt caught, like a mealy worm smashed at the center of their sight.

"Get off our case," Levi said. "It's not pot and we're not doing anything so terrible, so you don't have to tell Mom."

The way he spoke to her made Justice feel ashamed of herself. She stood there hanging her head and clutching her hands.

Levi took a last drag on the cigarette and put it out in an ashtray which already held two butts. The way he did that made him seem much older, separating him from her. Finally, she eased down next to the couch, hoping to close the gap between them.

"But if Mom ever found out—" she said, at last. "You know you oughtn't to smoke." Then, "Please make Thomas stop that drumming. I cannot stand so much noise!"

Looking very dramatic—pitiful, actually—she covered her ears. But truly the drumming hurt her in back of her eyes. And it made her insides feel full of jumping nerves.

"It's not noise," Levi said matter-of-factly. "It's full of

patterns." He did smile at her sympathetically.

Justice pouted back at him. "It's too loud and it makes my head hurt. Levi? Make him stop it."

"Oh, okay." At once, the drums ceased.

Surprised, Justice looked up to find Thomas putting away his cymbal brushes.

"It isn't noise, though," Levi said. "Noise is like—"

She watched, wide-eyed, as simultaneously her brothers got up. Levi took Thomas' place, taking drumsticks from a pocket on the side of the snare drum. He commenced beating the drum and working the bass. He hit the floor tom-tom and the cymbals. Levi filled the parlor with the worst confusion of sound Justice had ever heard.

The beats forming a drummer's logic had no order when he played them. He had so little sense of timing or rhythm that the pattern he'd spoken of before was completely missing.

"That's noise!" he shouted to Justice over the racket, stopping it as quickly as he had begun it.

He handed over the drumsticks to Thomas and got up from the stool.

"Take it easy," he told his brother, like a whisper. Justice heard.

Thomas drummed again, but with a gentle beat.

"Good," Levi said, under his breath. Again, Justice heard.

"You better come on and eat," he told her. "I'll fix it up for you."

She let him step around her and out of the room before she followed. And she wouldn't look around at Thomas for fear he might stare her down.

Something is new, she couldn't help thinking.

She left the parlor with Thomas' gentle drumming pursuing her.

Something is different. They got up at the same time when Levi went to play the drums. Did they?

And last night, she thought, when Thomas beat the kettledrums. Levi's hands twitching. Brother!

She stopped there in the hall between the parlor and the kitchen. Thinking back to lunchtime yesterday and Levi saying something like, I am Thomas sometimes.

They say identicals can sense and feel for one another.

And figuring out how Thomas and Levi might know things about each other beforehand was like thinking ahead of time. Or backward. Something.

Could she tell her mom? Justice wondered.

Tell her what? That they get up at the same time? That one of 'em's hands twitch?

Not even her mom was going to think there was anything funny about that. Justice wasn't sure *she* did, either. But one thing she did know for certain: Thomas never liked her getting in between him and Levi.

He likes having Levi either alone by himself or alone with him. He likes having me away from them both.

And she knew that Levi always tried to protect her from Thomas' meanness and temper.

What if he was to turn on Levi the way he does me and some of the boys?

And, quite suddenly, she realized that the one person Thomas never turned on, never had a fight with, was his brother.

Now, that has to be weird. But I don't know what it

means. I don't know anything, she thought anxiously. And slowly made her way to the kitchen, where she quietly seated herself at the table.

Back to the sink, Levi stood drinking a cup of iced cocoa as Justice sat down. He thought she looked forlorn this morning—peaked and tired, like she might be coming down with something.

"You sure you're wide awake this morning?" he asked Justice.

Maybe his mom hadn't noticed how peaked Justice looked, being away so much.

"Did you leave a part of you asleep back in your room?" he said, joking with her. Smiling at her, he drained his cup and then went about setting her breakfast before her.

She stared at her favorite brother. "You sure you're still you?" she said. Their conversation yesterday in the kitchen came to her. "Did you leave yourself in there drumming?"

There was a split second in which something ran scared in his eyes.

"You get so upset over nothing," he said, not quite looking at her. "Smoking in there, it wasn't my idea."

"That just makes it so much worse," she said. "Follow the leader."

"It's not like that at all," he said, and added: "Eat your egg."

"I don't want any egg."

"Come on, Tice, eat your breakfast," he urged. "That's a brand-new egg there. The other one Mom made got all shriveled in the warmer. I had to eat it myself."

Right then he seemed about as normal and nice as a brother could be.

She stared at the egg. Done perfectly and sunny-side-up,

78

it still wasn't a Grade A Large. It was small and almost round. There was a slice of whole-wheat toast next to it. Justice felt it. The whole-wheat was soggy with too much butter. It was also warm, so she ate it.

They were acting as ordinary as they ever had. She had to admit that earlier, in the parlor, even Thomas hadn't seemed too wild.

It was me that was wild, she thought glumly.

Levi was hurrying around now, talking to her while finding her a napkin, which he'd forgotten to place next to her plate. He poured her a large glass of tangerine juice.

"Or would you rather have some iced cocoa?" he asked her.

"No."

"But what I meant about smoking in there," he said. He stopped. They both listened. Justice quit chewing.

Drumming still went on in the parlor. There was an air of testing about it, the way it would sound when Thomas was studying and reading from drum notation. It stopped and started unexpectedly.

"I mean," Levi said, "Tom-Tom has to try anything once. He has to experiment around."

Justice eyed him, swallowing juice. "But *you* don't have to. So why did you do it?"

"I did have to," he said. "Because. Because he has this real mad stuff that gets caught in the stutter and can't come out."

She gazed up at him, shuffling nervously from one foot to the other beside the table. She knew her egg would be getting cold, but at once she forgot about it.

"What are you talking about?" she asked.

"I'm trying to explain it," Levi said. "Doing different

79

things all the time kind of eases the pressure for him. Just imagine what . . . what it's like not being able to . . . to say anything you want. That's why Tom-Tom drums. He . . . doesn't e-e-ever *stutter* wh-wh-wh-whe—as-long-as heee's *drumming!*"

Justice stared at him. The last piece of soggy toast she had in her hand dropped to the plate. She watched Levi cover his mouth, as though to hide the halting speech that came from it. His eyes suddenly flared and gleamed with the smirking presence of Thomas. As though in a dream, she saw Levi smack his own face with his free hand and reach for his eyes to press them closed. And he stood there with his hands covering his mouth and eyes. Dimly, Justice was aware that the sound of drumming had stopped again.

Stillness paraded down the hall and utter quiet entered the morning kitchen. It crept around the table to capture them unawares.

There was a muffled rasp from Levi. Then his hands fell to his sides as easy drumming in swing time began again in the living room. He slumped down into the chair across from her. He breathed heavily and looked limp and exhausted, but Justice saw no lurking presence in his eyes. What had she seen a moment ago?

She found herself on her feet, and for a long time she stood there, gripping the table edge.

"He drums to stop the stutter?" she asked.

Her voice seemed to clear the air. Levi sat straighter, but kept his face turned slightly away from her.

"At least," he said, "that's why he took it up in the first place." There was no halting sound to his speech now.

"Oh, I am awful dumb!" she said. A flash of memory

came to her. Thomas kicking furniture, bursting out with something mean. Being loud and beating on anything with the flat of his hands.

"You haven't been around him enough to notice," Levi said.

She recalled Thomas pounding his fist and spitting words at her. In the dim past when she was much younger, before Thomas ever played drums, he had seemed to pound and stomp his way through her life. And she had never suspected he might be trying to find a way out of his stutter.

Justice listened to the drumming from the parlor. She heard the cymbals' chim/chi-chim.

Thomas racing around, yelling his head off. But did he have to hurt somebody to get the words out?

She stood there staring fixedly at the table, and slowly she understood that this was not what she and Levi should have been talking about.

"You and Thomas," she said. "Levi, listen!" Whispering, forcing him by her urgency to look at her. "I get the feeling that the two of you— I get so scared the way you two seem—"

And she broke off as a warning so swift, so insistent, swelled in his eyes.

"You should be outside playing," he said hoarsely. He smiled wildly, then steadily at her. "Go on and ride your bike for an hour," he told her. "Maybe find somebody to play with."

Casually, he got up from the table and busied himself clearing away her dishes.

"This you call finished?" he said, staring at her plate, his voice somewhat louder than it needed to be. "You should've eaten the egg. I went to a lot of trouble."

"I'm sorry," she said.

"Never mind, nothing to be sorry for," he said. "I'll cook two or three more and make sandwiches out of them." He spoke bravely, but Justice noticed a quaver in the sound of his voice. "Thomas and I both like to eat cold eggs," he said.

She hated cold eggs. It was one more thing that separated her from them. Only a moment ago, she knew, she and Levi had somehow grown closer. She had grown older and they were together within some terrible, vague—she could not name what it was.

I can't keep it straight, she thought. Thomas doesn't stutter when he drums—that's something I didn't know. I just flat-out missed it. How could I have missed it?

And why had Levi actually sounded like Thomas stuttering? And covered his eyes and his mouth for some reason. Why did he do that? she wondered.

She moved out of Levi's way, standing leaning her shoulder on the doorjamb. Down the hallway, there was Thomas parading toward her.

Forever the spitting image of Levi. But Thomas was a stronger, louder image, she had to admit it. There was total life, total noise in the furious way he moved.

Coming at her, he gave her a screaming look before he chose to ignore her completely.

"Yeah, sure," Levi said, "go on out and play," as though he and Justice had been talking right then, "but don't stay away forever."

Thomas came on, passing by Justice. All at once, he spun around, slamming the flat of his hand on the doorjamb above her head.

"G-g-g-got thaaat old spuh-ider!" he said, grinning at the space above her.

She clung to the doorway. Thomas had frightened her speechless. But she knew better than to say anything. That's all he wanted, so he could pick on her.

She knew there was no spider.

Justice slid out of the doorway and managed to walk calmly down the hall.

"You didn't have to tease her like that," she heard Levi say, his voice low.

Thomas snickered. "Wh-whaaat's fer bre-breee—wh-ut's to eat?"

I'm dumb as they come, she thought, ashamed of herself for not realizing. But she was furious at Thomas and hurt by his meanness.

And found herself yelling, she couldn't help it: "Thomas? Guh-guh-oood buh-buh bye, stuh-stuh-stutter-rat!" Frantically, she ran from the house, slamming the door as hard as she could.

On the vicious sound of Thomas screeching at her.

I've done it now, she thought as she hurtled through the burning heat.

5

Outside is better than in. Better for running. Hiding, she thought.

She raced around the house to the backyard. She'd heard the side door open as she scrambled through the gate, and her brothers talking loud:

Levi saying anxiously, "She was only getting you back. You started it. Why you have to bother her for?"

Thomas answering, stammering, "IIII'm not g-g-gonna *hurt*-er!"

She ran for the thick line of osage trees on the far side of the field. There, in the high weeds and damp shadow, she hid herself as best she could. Pressing herself to the earth, she made a ball by hugging her knees to her chest and wrapping her arms around her legs.

The side door slammed shut. She heard the muffled sound of feet running aimlessly. She dare not breathe. It had to be Thomas searching for her. Oh, it was so wild of him to make such a big thing out of her teasing. But then, for a time, she heard no unusual sound. She didn't move, though, guessing that Thomas had become more cautious when he figured out where she would hide.

Justice closed her eyes and listened to the silence.

Something, she thought finally.

In the stillness of age-old trees, she became aware of a presence. It seemed to have the energy to unsettle the air near her. She could sense its touch along the weeds and low branches that shielded her. She couldn't say she was shocked or surprised. She simply accepted the presence as the nature of Thomas. And Justice knew at once how to protect herself.

She gathered herself within into one hard place. Small of size, the place was a rock.

The presence that was Thomas swept over the weeds, then fell to probe along their roots. It flowed along the rock, passed by and flowed back to range behind. It had searing rage and unnatural heat.

Thomas could not find Justice, although his presence was very close to the rock, hard with centuries.

I know you're in there, the presence seemed to say.

Aqueous stone. Timeless.

I'm the one growing stronger.

"You-you . . . youuu g-g-gotta come hhhome s-s-s . . . *sometime!*" Thomas said, his words exploding from some distance away. "III'll muh-muh, mmmake youuu *miserable!*"

Time upon time suspended. Somewhere, a door opened and slammed shut again, although at first Justice didn't recognize the sound as such. Sound had become meaningless, she had been so deep and hard within. But now she knew that stillness again surrounded her midst the hedge's armor. Cautiously now, she came back to the comfort and safety of the ancient trees.

Strained muscles ached her. Minutes passed as she painfully unclasped her hands to release her legs. She had little strength left to brush away ants and other insects crawling over her. But she did straighten full-length in the weeds, feeling that somehow she had triumphed. Dimly, she sensed she had done something odd, beyond the ordinary range of what was Justice, age eleven.

I hid myself from Thomas, that's what I did, she thought.

Her mind clicked on fully. And she was struck by waves of terror that shook her from head to foot.

Heard his head talking to me—I did! Him looking for me in the weeds, but using just his *mind*—can it be true?

She covered her face with her hands, turned on her side and pulled her knees up. In a moment, she was crying in heaving sobs.

Being not very big, Justice could not feel terror for long. She held her breath seconds at a time to calm herself. Soon, she was breathing somewhat easier, and wiped the tears from her eyes.

Not even a soul to help me figure this out, she thought. Levi's home, but I can't go back there. Thomas is sure to do something if I don't get away. Why can't he stand me to tease him? He sure teases me enough.

Justice considered which way was best to go. She was up and going the best way before she realized she had moved.

Stay real low. But I can stand, no one is able to see me here. Staying low because I'm still so scared.

She thought she heard a pulsebeat of drumming from the house.

Don't take a chance of him snagging you on his mind— get away!

Was it possible, she wondered, for a body to let go its mind like something silky? To let it sail out and have it fall over you?

Again, she felt terror rising and firmly forced it back.

Brother, why was he ever born!

Staying low, she made her way down the field within the

hedgerow. Thoughts racing with her heartbeat, she recalled hearing about her brothers being born. Tumbling images, memories. She didn't know exactly when she had heard. Justice had some trouble with time. Often, time carried her along so fast. Other moments, it hung around her and was slow going.

But her mom had said once that Thomas had been born first. Then Levi was born, about five hours later, as if he hadn't wanted to come into the world.

Because he knew the kind of trouble was lying there, Justice thought. Lying in wait for him.

Cautiously, she moved down the row. Eyes darting, she would suddenly swivel her head around to stare behind. She dreaded to find some silk curtain drifting after her. But, sensing there was no one, she crept on, making little sound.

Her mom telling her that, from early on, she and Justice's dad hadn't known which identical was Thomas and which was Levi.

Justice had never thought much about it. But now the idea made her pause there hidden in the trees.

From the time the boys were babies, Justice recalled her mom telling her. Her mom had them safe in the middle of her big bed, ready to dress them nice and sweet after their bath. Her mom saying she could always tell the boys apart. But for some reason, after she bathed them, she got the habit of tying different-colored ribbon around each one's ankle. Old, soft Christmas ribbon from a shoebox full of it. Red ribbon always for Thomas and yellow for Levi. Just as if the boys were pretty presents. Or maybe, her mom saying, maybe she wasn't as sure she could tell them apart as she liked to think.

Anyway, her mom had gone to get something for them

from the bathroom—she said she never did remember what it was she'd forgotten. Then the phone had to ring—wouldn't you know? And her mom swore she hadn't been on the phone long. Always she had the safety of the boys on her mind. And hurrying back to them, unaccountably afraid, she found one of them had rolled off the bed, or had crawled to the edge and over the side. Her mom saying, Thank goodness for some thick carpeting.

The other baby faced the foot of the bed on his stomach. Nine-month-old boys—her mom had left the both of them on their backs, side by side. The one on the bed had been screaming his head off. The one on the floor rocked back and forth, or up and down, on his hands.

Her mom grabbed up the babies. Holding them, squeezing them so close, she had become almost hysterical, she said. Out of fear she'd caused the one that had fallen to be injured. Of course, they were all right. She hadn't found a mark or a bruise on either one of them.

And she had cried, her mom had.

Because the red ribbon and the yellow ribbon lay tangled in a tiny clump on the bed.

Her mom saying, seeing the ribbon, what she thought she knew would identify one baby from the other simply vanished. She never again was certain that the baby she called Thomas was not Levi, or which one was born first.

Well, I know which one was born first, Justice thought now.

She shivered, going slowly down the row.

Thomas was the one born first, just so proud to lead and to lord it over everyone. But no sooner was she certain that Thomas could never be Levi than she recalled what had happened at lunch. The way Levi had seemed to change into Thomas right before her eyes.

Next, she realized again that moments ago she had become a rock.

Was I really?

And Thomas—no, not Thomas, but Thomas behind his eyes, bodiless, hunting her with . . . with his mind!

Justice was being careful now of sharp osage thorns growing out of the tree bark. She stepped high over horizontal branches. It was in the middle of such a high step that she had a sudden notion. She was almost—

Not alone.

With one foot raised as if to climb an invisible stair, she stood frozen. Listening. Not to the day around her, nor the creaking weight of old trees. She was not conscious of the wet heat and the sweet stickiness that the trees held and pressed in on her.

She was listening to herself inside. She had a notion of something with her, within her.

Wavering motion. She sensed an enormous tremor of light and dark just beyond the verge of her thinking. Something with her, within her.

It went away, whatever it had been, leaving a vast impression.

I'm so scared out here, she thought uneasily. She took a deep breath and tightened her insides against fear.

Trees made a dome above her, leaning over and into the field from the west property line. Volunteer osage saplings pitched back upon the old trees. Brittle and thick horizontal branches stretched across thirty feet of ground. They were about four feet above the earth, reaching out toward the young saplings and sunlight. These heavy branches were like braces between the young and old growth. Justice took great pleasure in playing follow the leader on them. Following and imitating an imaginary self, she had risked thorn wounds to walk the branches. Just playing. But not today.

She brushed off her clothing as she went along, sweeping her back with her arms to dislodge any insects still clinging to her. Under her blue jeans, she could feel pressure prints of stones and twigs on the skin of her knees from when she'd made herself into a rock. Such a short time had passed. She found herself clear down the field at the very end of the hedgerow. She took a sudden, last look behind her.

Arched trees. Shade and leaves, twisted branches and dappled light. A long, lovely row; a vaulted chamber. Standing there at the end of it, Justice had an inkling how old a place it was. Within it, time seemed suspended, quivering in uneven waves of heat. Here was her familiar hedgerow where so much that was strange had occurred.

Tomorrow, there'll be snakes hanging here, she thought, as all at once The Great Snake Race was on her mind. Shaped by the timeless osage row, the event was made small.

She turned away. At her feet was a broken-down fence separating the hedgerow from the Stevenson property right next to the Jeffersons'. Poison ivy entwined with rusted and flaking fragments of the fence. She took a leap over; made it. She cut left across the backyard, keeping her head down to avoid looking at the Duane Stevenson house in front of her. She hoped the Stevenson people hadn't seen her as she skirted their side of the Jefferson hedge.

'Course, by now they'd of gone to work, Justice thought.

Stevensons had no children. Just a quiet man and woman who left early in the day and came home at suppertime. They owned a long-haired house dog that would never grow big. It barked its head off whenever anyone approached the house. Justice could hear it yapping away now, just frantic, trapped behind the heat of closed windows.

She went on. With her head bowed and her knees bent slightly to make herself even smaller, she pretended she cut across others' land the way Dorian and the rest of the boys did most every day. For the times when she planned a visit to Mrs. Jefferson, she never came down the field. She would act as though she were going for a bike ride.

And maybe even go for a short one, Justice thought.

And skirting the south side of town, she would head back to Dayton Street by the westward end.

She reached the street now, on the sidewalk between the Stevenson and Jefferson houses. She breathed easier, for the fact was it made her nervous to trespass the shaded privacy between homes.

A few paces up the walk, she turned left to enter the Jefferson yard. She ducked in behind their front hedge, which was almost as tall as she. Dusty from the street, it was turning brown and skimpy in places, dying from dry weather.

A dust bowl is coming, maybe, Justice thought. A sky bowl full of sand, coming to smother the cattle (what cattle?) and us, too.

She took the short, curved walk up to the front stoop and saw Dorian Jefferson at the picture window. She didn't know how many times she had found him there like that. He never seemed to be looking out. Seeing her coming, he pressed his face against the windowpane. Mouth and nose flattened, he bugged out his eyes and appeared to be locked in the window, sucking glass.

91

She gave him a pained, superior look. You're not scaring a soul. You're just getting the glass messy.

Otherwise, neither of them bothered to greet the other. She couldn't say whether they were friends.

He never lets on I come here. Thomas would have teased me if he'd mentioned it.

Maybe they were friends. Secret friends.

Her heart beat faster. She watched Dorian leave his post at the window as she stepped up on the stoop.

Dorian's mother was a secretive person if ever Justice had seen one. Some kind of caution she had come to share with Dorian. Mrs. Jefferson would seem to let Dorian slip from her mind. She never seemed to pay attention to him, and this didn't bother him at all. But she never for an instant forgot about Justice's brothers.

"Watching they every move," she would tell Justice. "Somebody got to."

There was another world where Mrs. Jefferson lived. Justice could feel herself being drawn into it once again.

Most houses this time of day were closed tight against the hot weather. The Jefferson house was no exception. When Justice went to open the screen door, she found it locked.

Should-a known, she thought.

The screen was caked with dust. She saw that the entire front of the house was dust-covered, as was the hedge.

You don't see it at first, she thought. Sure does look like the dust bowl is spilling over everything.

A moment later, Dorian opened the door and unlocked the screen. She tried to get by him into the house, but he was too quick for her. He thrust out a short-handled broom, which she took from him. She couldn't recall having seen the broom before; yet she knew exactly what was to be done with it.

Do it and get it over with. She sighed, turning around, facing the yard and hedge. Just get it done.

Justice went down to the hedge opening where the sidewalk up to the Jefferson home began. There she felt compelled to sweep backward toward the stoop. She hoped none of the neighbors would see her as she swept the broom across the walk in front of her backing feet.

"Because of the Child and Child," Mrs. Jefferson had said. Justice had the impression that Dorian's mother had given this as a reason for the need of sweeping. Mrs. Jefferson never said Thomas' and Levi's names. She would say One Child for Thomas and Two Child for Levi. Or Them. Or she said Child and Child. Justice, as she swept, said Child and Child over and over again to herself. She could see how thoroughly it left her out of things.

"Because nobody know how much of Them is tracking you." Justice knew Mrs. Jefferson had told her this. "So sweep away the footprints, you, so Child and Child cannot follow."

Justice did as she had been told.

There had been a time when she believed Leona Jefferson was some kind of crazy woman. But gradually she had grown accustomed to Mrs. Jefferson's peculiar ways. They still appeared odd to what Justice knew as order and routine; yet they made a kind of sense within the world of the Jefferson household.

Now Justice swept the broom up to the stoop and climbed backward up the steps. She thought of her own house, now hidden by the Jefferson place. Her own house was the best house and the one she loved. At once, Thomas was on her mind—never was he out of it for long—and the way she had hidden herself in the hedgerow. She quaked with dread.

I have to tell someone, she thought, and pulled herself together.

The front door opened. Justice turned to face it, still clutching the broom. Dorian held open the screen and took the broom from her. She stepped forward and entered this house like no other.

There was no entrance hall or foyer in Dorian's house. A visitor stepped across the threshold and was simply within. There wasn't time for Justice to rearrange her mind's eye from the bright, searing outdoors to this damp and cool interior. But she reminded herself about the powdery dust outside, how the screen door had been caked with it. The dust pressed against the frame of the picture window, rising in the corners like the sands in an hourglass. Fragments of dust had filled the air, like a town's dry gossip, which goes unnoticed until it begins to chafe and burn.

Now Justice stood in the Jefferson house surrounded by carpeted floors of evergreen and the cabbage green of pictureless walls. A huge floor-to-ceiling mirror made portraits of whoever stood where Justice was standing.

Clay pots of crinkled ivy were crammed on end tables. And the tables, in turn, crowded the spring-green couch on which Dorian sat with hands tightly folded, waiting for Justice.

She sensed that the plants welcomed her, that they understood her as they did Dorian and his mother. She felt them empty her of all the silliness of her years. All of the nonsense.

No, please! she begged them. *I want to stay myself.*

The green of plants crowded her vision and gripped her mind. She was given a keener awareness. She became a receiver.

Justice was prepared.

And found herself seated on the couch next to Dorian.

"I never knew I moved from the doorway," she told him, surprised.

"Justice, you," he said evenly. But he looked apprehensive and gave her a guarded little smile.

"I been here long?" she asked him.

"Not too long. You only just come in a minute ago."

"You sure of that?" she asked.

"Maybe you been here a little while, but not long," he assured her. Holding himself still and straight on the couch, he was unwilling to look at her more than a few seconds at a time.

She folded her hands, feeling them pulse and tremble. She leaned back on the couch and closed her eyes, only to see a swell of green behind her eyelids. They fluttered open again.

"You can let it be," softly Dorian reminded her. "Nothing's not going to get you hurt in here."

"I know that," she mumbled, and was quiet before she said, "Your dad's still asleep."

No need for Dorian to answer. His dad slept through the morning on into afternoon so that he could be alert for his night shift at his job.

Justice had the sensation that time wavered green, and changed. She sensed that it would escape. She often had trouble keeping it.

There was an arch between the front room where she and Dorian were sitting and the kitchen and dining area. She could see through the arch to the back door, which was curtained in aqua lace with a green blind beneath. To the left of the door was the round dining table where the Jeffersons ate their meals. Only half the table was visible behind the wall separating the two rooms. Justice knew who had to be seated there at the table, out of view.

A wind came up in the front room, causing plant runners to skittle over the floor like crabs. Dust was shaken by the wind from the fronds of a wild palm.

There can't be wind here, she thought.

But the wind lifted her with Dorian at her elbow, steering her. It sailed her from the couch through the arch. There were voices with her on the wind. She sensed they came from miles and miles away. Insistent voices echoing in the new clarity of her mind. One voice was particularly at a loss.

Justice whirled on the wind. "Where—how far away are you?"

She knocked into the dining table in the kitchen. She could see only green. The confused sound of voices was like thunder swelling and rolling in.

Hands from across the table grasped her arms. The hands trembled with fear, but still they firmly held her. At once, she and Dorian were seated at the table, side by side. The wind escaped under the back door and through cracks of the house. The voices died away to a hum, like the sound of a refrigerator.

"Can you hear me, Justice, you?" said Leona Jefferson. "Baby Justice, come on back now."

"I was sailing!" Justice said, shocked. She had difficulty seeing through a green mist. Her heart pounded, shaking the table. A surge of frightening beats filled the house.

"Mama!" she heard Dorian cry out in terror.

"Shhhh!" Leona's voice saying, "She's not going to hurt anything. We can keep it in, but you can't be afraid and you have to concentrate!"

Hands touched Justice's face, smoothed back her hair. They pressed hard on each side of her head at the temples. She felt herself quake inside and she wanted so much for the hands to make her feel safe. But they were like so many flies. She was able to knock them away without even moving.

"Mama?" Dorian whispering.

"Shhhh!"

"How did I do that?" Justice asked. "It's scaring me—make it go away!"

Hands flew back, pressing her head again.

"Stop it!" Justice cried out. Then, quite suddenly, she gave in: "No, let them be. Let the hands alone."

"That's right," Leona said soothingly. "We got to keep it in, mostly. Let it out a little at a time."

Justice turned her head this way and that; the hands turned also. Wherever she looked, objects moved, slid and jumped, and rustled in a sudden wind.

"I thought all the wind had gone," she said. No one answered.

But hands were helping to calm her down, although a huge pounding continued in the room. She couldn't imagine what it was. Her own heart beat now—tinka-tink, tinka-tink—racing small and insignificant. Yet, ever so slowly, the pounding diminished. Perhaps the hands absorbed it. They did seem to draw it off, Justice felt, the way creeks catch and hold the run-off of water from a flash of hard rain. The hands were so soothing.

She sensed the room settle down. The three of them were seated comfortably at the round table. Justice and Dorian were closest to the arch, with Leona Jefferson across from them.

There were no hands touching Justice. She hadn't noticed when they stopped pressing her temples. Now she saw in the center of the table a large round pan some three inches deep. She stared at the familiar-looking tin, but found no memory of it.

"You practice on the small things," someone said. "That's how you learn."

"Huum? Is that you, Leona?" Justice asked. "Why is it sometimes you sound just like some teacher?" She sat with her chin in her hands, looking into the tin. It was full of smooth white sand. There were little piles of yellow, blue and red sand on top, like bright buttes or cones.

"Baby child," Leona said, "I can sound any way I need to sound, you know that."

"Uuum." Justice felt fine and ever so relaxed, as though her eyes were closed. "You are the Sensitive, aren't you? But I don't know—"

"You *do* know, honey," Leona said soothingly. "Why you want to fight it so long and hard?"

"Fight it?" Justice said.

"Because there's not only the one kind, like Child and Child," Leona said.

"My identical brothers," Justice said.

"There is born mind and mind. There is born a child and power!"

"Oh, no," Justice said.

"Powerful Justice!" said Leona, her voice wavering with feeling. "And no one might not never know. But the Sensitive always know."

"No," Justice said again.

"Without me to bring you together with it, you wouldn't have a chance."

"Together. It makes me so afraid," Justice said. There was a thin veil of green behind her eyes. She sensed it would be with her so long as she stayed inside this house.

"One day, everything will change for you," Leona told her, "but you mustn't let anyone know for a while."

"I'm so afraid of Thomas," Justice said.

"And not the other one, the Number Two Child?"

"Levi wouldn't hurt a soul," Justice said.

"You know that for sure?"

"Yes. But Thomas can hurt and hurt somebody," Justice said.

"You'll have to beat him one day, and beat him for good," the Sensitive said.

"I don't want to hurt anyone," Justice told her.

"You won't, baby, not unless you have to."

"Look," said the Sensitive. "Look at the sand."

Justice and Dorian leaned low over the table so that their eyes were level with the rim of the pan. She willed herself and Dorian inside the pan, where the white sand became for them a vast, arid land of heat. Their size had diminished; they were made small.

Brilliant-colored buttes rose like isolated mountains to tower over them out of the surrounding white sand. They skirted the red butte, holding hands. Standing still, their hands lifted in the air and their arms stiffened, as a divining rod.

Justice was holding hands with someone else on her right. She sensed it was Levi, although he was not visible to her. But their arms stiffened also, rodlike again.

Clasped hands of the three of them pointed at the butte. At once, they heard the immense, the deafening grind of a mountain moving. They moved the red butte over the sand. But the enormous gap it left behind showed them nothing useful.

They moved a yellow butte. And three hundred feet below the gap left by it, they found what they needed.

Justice withdrew herself and Dorian from the pan. And again they leaned low at the rim. The experience had left Dorian trembling from head to foot. His shoulders jerked uncontrollably and his breath came in shallow pants.

"Concentration," said the soft, determined voice of the Sensitive. She placed a hand on Dorian to calm him. Soon, he was quiet at Justice's side.

"Must I concentrate?" Justice asked the Sensitive. When there was no answer, she sighed and did as she was told.

"Your sight must be no wider than a pin," said Leona. "Use only the right eye."

Justice covered her left eye with her palm and concentrated on the white sand.

"Now. Move the colored sands where they belong."

She first moved the red butte.

"Careful!" whispered the Sensitive.

Justice refocused a pinpoint of sight out of her right eye. She lifted the miniature cone of sand. Dorian, with his weaker sight, helped to hold it steady as she reduced and directed the energy she needed. Next, she took over from Dorian to move the red butte into place above its gap.

Then Justice worked the yellow sand cone, setting it smoothly down and leaving no trace of the hole it had made, nor the fresh water beneath it.

The whole time, she had the feeling of motion and power, of clean strength swelling to engulf them. It frightened her and it filled her with awe.

"You did the yellow cone real good," said the Sensitive. "Now, Baby Justice, tear the red apart."

100

Justice separated the red cone into particles and swirled them into a red sand devil.

Dorian let out a sharp cry, and drew back in fear.

"Shhh!" the Sensitive cautioned him.

A furious red cloud danced over the miniature desert. Easily, Justice had made it a tiny cyclone, using no more energy than it took an eyelash to twitch. When told to tear the red apart, she could do it and add her own creation of the dance as well. Justice sensed her power to live in each particle and that each lived in her.

The red cyclone was following her thoughts, but it did not stop its swirl.

Then, suddenly, Justice commanded it merely by thinking: *Quit your dance.*

The cyclone hung still above the sand. Justice could see each of its red sand dots that made circles—so tiny and glowing. Each had obeyed her command and was at ease, waiting.

"You did that on your own?" spoke the Sensitive, her voice full of wonder.

"I did it," Justice said. She swallowed several times, for her mouth had gone dry.

"Can you do other things with it, on your own?"

"Yes. I can," Justice said.

"Can you move the blue cone while holding the red cyclone still?" whispered the Sensitive. The kitchen was still, utterly, as Justice thought.

She needed only to remind herself of the blue butte for it to become alert to her as the other cones had.

"I can move it," she said, and moved the blue over the sand toward the rigid red cyclone. "Now I can do with them without even looking at them."

She closed her eyes, lifting the blue cone with just her

thought. She whirled a ring of the red cyclone and she held the yellow peak at bay. She poured blue sand over the red cyclone until the single moving ring grew heavy and fell to the ground.

"I didn't tell you to do any of this," said the Sensitive.

Justice opened her eyes, staring at the sand. "You're thinking I'm changed," she said.

"Yes," said the Sensitive cautiously.

"I am still changing," Justice said.

"I think you must be pulling together inside," said the Sensitive.

"I don't want any of this," Justice told her.

"It's not to be your choice," said the Sensitive.

"I want it to go away."

"It won't. You will have to live with it, and we have to prepare you," said the Sensitive. "There's no other way."

"But where does it come from? What *is* it?" Justice asked, in anguish. As she spoke, a part of her kept the sands in place and was quick to strengthen them if they seemed to falter. It was this part of her that spread sadness out over the miniature sands.

"We don't know the answer to that," the Sensitive was saying, "and we may never know."

"Mrs. Jefferson, I'm tired, I want to go home," Justice said.

"Soon," said the Sensitive.

Justice felt relieved. She removed the blue sand from the red and poured it back into the shape of a blue butte. She moved it to the far side of the pan, where it belonged, and put back the rigid red cyclone in its own form and place.

An unspoken moment in which the Sensitive entered Justice's thoughts and there read the trouble with Thomas.

102

She let Justice know she had been there.

"So what about him, then?" Justice asked her.

"I'll take care of him, that's not hard," Mrs. Jefferson said. "You'll remember none of this, as always. Oh, and it's a great power you've shown here today! And now you have the will to protect yourself and the Number Two Child."

"Levi," said Justice. "I will protect him."

"Yes, you will watch out for him for his own protection. And when it's time," said the Sensitive, "you'll remember everything. You'll know what to do."

"I want to go home," Justice said. "I want my mom." But she made no move to leave.

" 'Course you do, baby." Mrs. Jefferson was her own self again, completely. A woman, somewhat odd, who lived her life down the field from Justice.

Still seated at Justice's side was Dorian, like a ragamuffin child, always full of nerves. Yet, inside this house, no matter how much Justice's extraordinary power might frighten him, he was her friend, and faithful to his mother.

Justice felt as if she were coming in from a place beyond herself. She watched Mrs. Jefferson take a large bowl of fruit salad from the refrigerator and mix in whipped cream from a smaller bowl. Next, Mrs. Jefferson spooned the fruit mixture into separate bowls, serving them to Justice, Dorian and herself. Once again, the three of them sat together at the table, this time eating delicious fruit.

"Uuum! I like the taste so much," Justice said. By the time she had finished, she was herself again. Looking all around, seeing the kitchen as if for the first time. The last thing she remembered clearly was getting up from the couch with Dorian. She suddenly felt confused. In alarm,

Dorian turned from her to his mother.

Leona was quick to sense Justice's uneasiness and entered Justice's mind without her knowing, as was her Sensitive's ability. She wiped away partial memories of power and gave Justice a sense of peaceful quiet. She wove through Justice's memory a calm conversation at the table. Justice would believe they had talked over her problems and that there was now nothing to worry about.

Leona was feeling confident. She had been summoned to live in this community. Her unceasing ability to weave her will through the mystery of time and space had uncovered power here. Eagerly, she had come to live here, only to discover surprisingly less power, full of petty anger and cruelty. Yet it had been power all the same, and it belonged to the Number One Child called Thomas. And she sensed there was true power somewhere deeply submerged. She had waited, scanned and searched. Finally, she had uncovered it, the source for good. Just today, she had been able to help Justice become a rock without frightening her unduly. Here in this room she had taught the child a valuable lesson in directing power and conserving its energy.

Leona allowed Justice to sense the interval that had passed, the length of a good visit.

"What time is it?" Justice asked abruptly.

"Oh, about quarter past two," Mrs. Jefferson told her.

"I gotta be going," Justice said. "My mom'll be coming home."

"Glad you came by," said Mrs. Jefferson. "I missed you this week, what with y'all preparing for a snake race."

"How'd you know about that!" Justice could hardly speak, she was so shocked. And turned an accusing look on Dorian.

104

He fidgeted nervously, staring from her to his mother. "You think nobody can hear the Number One Child with his drums in the field?" Leona said. "He can yell loud enough for the whole town to hear him. But I don't guess else folks take the time. I happen to get a kick out of spying."

"Well," Justice said, "you won't tell on us, will you?"

"Not much to tell, even if I cared to," Leona said. "Y'all chil'ren have to dare the jeopardy." She smiled primly.

Such a queer sort of parent Mrs. Jefferson was, Justice couldn't help thinking. It was funny how sometimes she spoke with a Southern accent and other times— Justice couldn't recall exactly how she did sound at other times.

Different, though, she thought, and eased herself up from the table. Dorian and his mother stared at her as she turned and headed for the front door.

"Bye," she called back to them.

Through the room of plants, so green. Painstakingly, Dorian had taught her what all of the green things were called. She still remembered them now. And seeing the plants quieted her completely. As if they were calling her, paying their respects with their runners:

You may sit here awhile. Rest, hide here as long as you want.

Ever so slightly, Justice shook her head at them, pressing in on her on all sides. She didn't want to stare at them, nor look in the mirror, where she was sure to see her own portrait.

She looked, she couldn't help herself. Standing in the mirror was a hungry child whose mouth had gone dry. Seconds passed before she realized she stared at her own reflection, it looked so like someone familiar, but older.

105

"Goodbye," she said to the reflection, and turned away.

Justice slammed out of the house into sudden, glaring heat and high wind out of nowhere. For a moment, she thought it was raining in the sunlight. But what was hitting her face and bare arms were fine particles, much like sand.

"This stuff'll get all in my hair," she told herself. She ran for the open field and home. And never once felt the need to protect herself in the safety of the hedgerow.

6

She was inside the house without knowing how she had got there, or what she had thought about on the way. Her mom always did say that, at any time, anyone of her family could get an attack of the "vagues" and not know where they were going or coming from. Justice guessed that was her problem. And she had no recollection that she feared Thomas; but, rather, there was a shape of a suggestion that she respected him and his talent for drumming. It was a different feeling from the shimmering warmth she would always feel for Levi. She had erected a barrier between herself and Thomas which surrounded her like a wall. She would be able to see over it. Thomas might see her looking, but he wouldn't be able to come closer to her than the barrier.

She found Thomas behind his drums in the parlor. Heat lay trapped on dust streaks of sunbeams. The room was bathed in stark light where the only suggestion of shadow was in the form of the drummer. He beat the snare and the floor tom-tom with his brushes. Every once in a while, he used a key on a long chain to skim the edge of his cymbals. This made a mysterious, hissing sound, like a spray, a flash, of tiny bells.

Thomas' head bowed low over the drums. Barefooted, he wore jeans and was bare to the waist, working up a sweat. His eyes were dark and liquid bright, regarding her.

"Hi," she said breathlessly, heading for her room. But she couldn't help stopping in front of him to watch and listen. "I always did like that sweet sound of them brushes," she told him. Smiling, showing teeth, she fairly disarmed him.

"Where you been all this time?" he asked, only half grudgingly.

"All over. I been everywhere running around," she said. She lied without bothering herself about it. It was what had to be done from behind the barrier between them.

Standing close at his elbow, she stared at the drums and cymbals as his brushes made them whisper. The combination of instruments sounded—Swee su-swee/Swee su-swee/su-su—over and over. Gradually, Thomas altered the rhythm to a jaunty beat. Justice soon noticed its sly amusement.

"How'd you ever do something like that?" she said. She laughed, delighted.

"I have to finish up my practice now," he said. Thomas seemed almost shy with her. His expression was guarded, but it was not unkind.

"Where's Levi?" she asked suddenly. Not waiting for him to reply, she turned and bounded away toward the kitchen.

No one there, just a clean, neat space, with cupboards closed, chairs pulled in at the table and all dishes put away. The radio on the counter mumbled low. She went over, flicking the dial around. Justice didn't bother turning up the sound. By listening closely—it was like fine-tuning her hearing—she could make sense out of the mumbling. She heard music, then switched to a soothing voice on local FM. But rather than stand there, she decided she'd be more comfortable in her room. So she cradled the small pink radio against her and worked the plug loose. "There." And brushed crumbs of toast from the top of the radio. Evidently, Levi had missed wiping them away. She stood there, undecided about something. Her thinking was all scattered, waiting for her mom to come home, waiting for the day to turn around and be over. Why was she waiting the day through, with nothing more than that on her mind?

Who'd buy such a pink radio? was what broke through random thoughts and a distinct echo in her head of the soothing radio voice before she had pulled the plug on it.

She knew no one in the house would buy a thing like that. One day, her dad had to have brought it home from work. He was always bringing home things from small jobs when folks couldn't find the money to pay him. From some broken-down little house somewhere, with fanciful carved eaves that had to be repaired.

Her dad carved wood as good as he sized and chipped stone. But he never liked woodworking. He took such jobs in wood only when big stone jobs were scarce.

So he did the job, Justice decided, and he gave it more of his time than he should have. Because he liked doing any repair work to perfection.

And after the first day, knowing that folks couldn't afford to pay for the care he'd taken. So he did it right anyhow.

And they pay him with what they have which is worth something to them.

"This funny little pink radio," she told herself. "It would be nice if we could trade things back and forth when we needed things. And not use money at all. Why in the world am I taking this radio to my room?"

Justice felt as if she had muddy water on the brain. Something was almost thick up there. Oozing around, she couldn't see through it. She had trouble remembering what she was doing.

Guess I'm excited over the snake race—

She sucked in her breath.

The snake race!

Clutching the radio tightly: How could you forget something like that? What's wrong with me today?

Where'd I put my knapsack for the snake!

"Levi!" Justice yelled at the top of her lungs and headed out of the kitchen.

No response from Levi. But she knew he had to be around. He was forever around the house.

Bet he has his earphones on, she thought.

When Levi listened to symphony, his earphones shut out Thomas' drumming and Justice, too.

Well, who cares? I can find the knapsack myself.

Thomas no longer drummed in the parlor. She wasn't surprised he'd left. And something else.

The plants are gone—are they? I seem to remember a lot of green all over.

There was an intense imprint of Thomas surrounding his drums. She sensed this on the stifling light of the room. She stood stock still, sensing a rust color glowing to a heated red on the cymbal brushes. Exposed rust color commenced to fade where Thomas had touched things all around the room.

Faint brownish footprints led from the parlor to the back hall and bedrooms. Justice recognized other footprints as pale yellow and knew they belonged to Levi. Turning to see behind her, she found her own footprints going and coming, patterned with blue light. For an instant, Justice fought against the suggestion that she should not be afraid.

110

She struggled to understand that seeing the impossible, the invisible, had to be something shocking. But the moment of reason passed. Peace and calm came over her; she accepted tranquilly whatever would come next.

Telltale footprints dissolved. Glancing around the room, she discovered little if anything that was different. What had been extraordinary sank beneath the murky fluids of her brain. By the time she reached her room and played around with the radio a bit, she had lost her potent awareness. Justice had seen nothing unusual.

Mrs. Douglass came home at a quarter past four to what seemed at first an utterly silent house. Her arms were filled with books, purse and groceries. And kicking the door closed behind her, she plunged into suffocating heat.

"My Lord, who took the screens out?" she said, seeing the screens in a pile on the floor beneath the parlor windows. She paused. Barely audible was music which she guessed was the radio playing somewhere. Listening hard, she heard a muffled pounding which slowly she recognized as Thomas beating his sticks on a padded block he used for practicing. She headed for the kitchen; on her way, she dumped groceries and everything else she had been carrying on the dining-room table.

"Thomas? Levi!" she called. But not loud enough. She hadn't the strength in all of the heat—it had been a long day. She turned back to the parlor, where she forced the windows up, the screens in, and rubbed her hands free of the dirt and dust from the windows.

Anger flared in her—at the dirt, the messy room, pillows on the floor, and the distinct, stale odor of smoke. But she calmed down, realizing she had no right to expect them, at home all day, to be as neat as pins.

But to close up the house like this!

Standing in front of the windows, she felt the heat pour in. It was fresh air, even if it was hot air.

They probably thought it would be cooler.

She smoothed back her damp, curly hair and was surprised to find it gritty with dirt.

It was windy today, she thought absently, and headed for the bedrooms.

She stopped first at the closed door of the boys' room, where the muffled pounding continued. Mrs. Douglass knocked hard, then paused before she opened the door.

She was struck by the brilliant light of day as she entered the room. The boys were at opposite ends from one another. Knowing they were sons, identical brothers, she was nevertheless startled at seeing double. So full was she of her own day and of being detached from this life for a while.

In the room there was a stronger odor of smoke.

Won't they ever open a window? Why must they confront me with this?

She glanced around, but saw no cigarettes or ashtray. Anger flared again. She felt a confusion of needs and obligations.

I'll get things in order again. I'll not go to school next fall, Mrs. Douglass thought.

"There are window fans in the garage," she told them, speaking hurriedly. "I want you both to get them out by the weekend, clean them and put them in the windows. This is ridiculous. This house doesn't have to be so hot."

Stopping herself, she struggled against further argument. This was no way to come home and greet them. It was almost time to start dinner. When would there be time for them to fool around together again?

112

The boys stared at her. Levi, across the room, was plugged into his earphones. His head moved slowly in rhythm with sounds she couldn't hear.

"Lee, will you open that window?"

He got up and opened the window, and sat down again. Not exactly smiling at her. How had he heard her? He hadn't, probably, she thought, but had recognized a few words as her lips moved.

Thomas sat drumming at his practice block. He slowed the beat as his mother turned to him.

"IIIII s-see M-m-mama is hhhome," he said, holding the sticks still as he spoke.

"Yes. Hello, Tom-Tom," she said. "How's everything?"

"F-f-fine. Eh-ehveryth-thing's ooo-k-k-kay." Again, the sticks had not moved.

He had deliberately held them still so he would stutter at her, Mrs. Douglass thought. Today he was angry at her, she could tell by the way he showed no expression. And perhaps today he blamed her for his stutter. Or maybe she was reading something into nothing. Feeling guilty again for being away.

Maybe there was something odd going on today. Something in the way Lee over there held himself in and didn't take his eyes off his brother.

"Where's Ticey?" Mrs. Douglass asked abruptly, turning to Levi.

"Iiiin-er r-room," Thomas answered.

"You can't be sure about that, can you, with your door closed?" She didn't wait for a reply. "I wish both of you wouldn't close her out so. You're not much older. You could include Ticey in, sometimes."

Thomas said nothing, but began beating his sticks on the block. A long, silent look passed between him and Levi.

Levi took off his earphones. They dangled over his shoulder.

"Hi, Mom," he said, as though she'd just now come in. "Justice is in her room, listening to the radio. We've been keeping track of her, honest."

Mrs. Douglass leaned against the door. She was hot and tired, with nerves tightening her insides. "You must be a mind-reader," she told him, "hearing what I say—with those earphones on?"

He laughed at her kidding. Did she imagine it; was his grin too wild?

"I turned the sound down when you came in," he said reasonably, "so I could hear you and the music, too."

"Well, that's a relief," Mrs. Douglass said.

"Uh-uh," Thomas said, beating his sticks in lightning rhythm, but ever so gently. It amazed her how completely his stutter left him when he beat on anything.

"Lee can blow minds," Thomas continued. "Blows them out like blowing out candles—we both can."

Levi seemed to pale. He looked stunned. "Tom-Tom, you weirdo. He's being a weirdo," he said softly.

"Nope. It's true," Thomas said to his mother.

Mrs. Douglass stared from one to the other. "So how do you blow minds?" she asked Thomas, but kept her gaze on Levi.

"Any way we want," Thomas said. "Mostly, we just read them. Sometimes we burn them and blow them out."

"I won't ask whether burning hurts," she said.

"No. It doesn't," Thomas said. "But the burnee gets the impression there's a fire close by."

"Neat," said Mrs. Douglass and had to smile.

Thomas gave her a pleasant, warm smile back, the same one Levi had given her before.

114

"That's the kind of thing he tells people," Levi said. "He puts it on thick and they believe it, some of them."

"I bet they do," said Mrs. Douglass. Again, she saw a long, silent look pass between the boys. For an instant, it appeared as if Thomas was the one with earphones on his shoulder, so positive was she that she had seen Tom-Tom's darkly amused expression on Lee's face.

She had no time to think about it. Thomas was saying, "Why do you think we never played games like other kids?"

"I thought you had," Mrs. Douglass said.

"And we did," Levi said.

"No, we didn't," Thomas said.

"We did, too!"

"Nope. You ever remember us playing much with cards?" he asked Levi.

"Sure! We played once in a while, just like all kids. Only, you never liked playing and you would find some way to spoil the fun!"

Thomas beating his drum in a blur of sticks, ever so softly. "Yeah," he said. "Playing Bid Whist, Tonk and Spit in the Ocean. We played once or twice. And you remember how we never could figure any of it out?"

"No, I don't remember we couldn't figure it out."

"One time," Thomas went on, "somewhere around age eight or nine. On some rainy Saturday afternoon, playing outside with some kids. Two packs of cards, one missing five cards and the other, twenty."

"Oh, man," Levi said. He glanced at his mom and then away, seeing that she was absorbed in Tom-Tom's story.

"So we put together a working deck from the two packs," Thomas said. "And we played a long time with a kid explaining the games to us. We played for hours."

"This is going to be a very long story," Mrs. Douglass said, amused.

"This isn't no story," Thomas said.

"It's pure, bareface lie," Levi said, forcing himself to remain calm. But his face was pale and tight. And Thomas seemed to enjoy greatly the effect he was having on his brother.

"Hurry it up," Mrs. Douglass said, "I have kitchen duty yet to do."

"Nothing much more to tell," Thomas said. He beat with only one stick—pah-ta/tah, pah-ta/tah—with the other at rest at his side. "We couldn't get the point, is all."

"You mean," Mrs. Douglass said, "you and Levi understood how the games were played, but you couldn't figure out why you would win or lose?"

"We couldn't get the *point,*" Thomas said carefully. "Because we knew what cards everybody else had and we knew what each other had."

"Wow," Mrs. Douglass said.

"So we just figured the other kids knew our cards, too."

"Oh, he is weird. Weird!" Levi said. He seemed to have gotten hold of himself and was looking at Thomas as though the whole thing were the worst kind of put-on.

"You knew if one of the kids held an ace or a king," said Mrs. Douglass.

"Or anything," Thomas said. "We just figured they could read our hands, too. So we never got the point of the games. We never figured we had a gift and they didn't."

Mrs. Douglass smiled, laughed once before she said, "So when did you find out you had the gift of card-reading and no one else had it?"

"And mind-reading, too," Thomas said.

116

"And mind-reading," she added.

"Oh, it dawned," he said. "And it scared Lee just about to death. That's why we stopped playing cards. Actually, it's more like I do the reading and funnel the information to him. He's got an opening in his brain which I can put things in."

Mrs. Douglass grinned at Levi: "A hole in the head!" But Levi wasn't amused. He looked disgusted and jammed his earphones back on. The next minute, he had taken them off, unwilling to miss any of the conversation.

Mrs. Douglass had turned back to Thomas. She wondered fleetingly why he had told this particular, very imaginative story. Why now, at this moment on this day just like so many others?

"Tom-Tom," she began, searching for the proper words, "I think that at times there may be something unusual between you and Lee."

"Mom . . . " Levi interrupted. "We're the same as anybody else. Tom-Tom is just putting on!"

"There's nothing to get so upset about," she said, her voice gentle and persuasive. "It's not strange for children to show the kind of ability you two seem to have. And especially when the children are identicals. It happens because young people have a natural open-mindedness. They might accept the unusual where an adult would not. Furthermore, this type of gift is known to disappear naturally with the end of childhood."

Thomas stared at her. He no longer beat on his practice block.

"There are tests for this ability, Tom-Tom," Mrs. Douglass said. "It wouldn't be difficult to go somewhere and have you and Lee tested. There's a card game that tests for telepathy, clairvoyance and precognition. Five hits in a 'run' of twenty-five cards is considered chance.

"But—and, Tom-Tom, this is interesting—" Mrs. Douglass said, "hits of much less or more *both* demonstrate *psychic* ability. . . ." The word hung in the air, the first time that any of them had mentioned super- or extra-sensory functioning of the mind. And they were all aware of it.

Thomas' cold and steady gaze bore into his mother as she left off speaking. "Yyyouuu know a-a-lot about it. Youuu must've st-stu-studied it. Whu-why?"

Mrs. Douglass didn't answer at once.

"Why do you bring up this story now?" she said, finally, to Thomas. "Why haven't you told it before?"

Thomas didn't answer. He ducked his head, beating his sticks again. "We played other games," he said, changing the subject. "Maybe we didn't play much cards, but we sure did play a lot of blind man's buff. We played it with Pic—I mean, with Ticey, too. She loved playing it."

"Another story," Mrs. Douglass said, "and you didn't answer my question."

But again Thomas ignored her. "The other kids thought Justice was a spoiled brat of a cheat," he said. "But I knew better because I tied that blindfold over her eyes myself every time. She couldn't see a thing.

"Blind Justice," Thomas added, grinning dreamily at his mom.

Mrs. Douglass felt suddenly that she must sit down. The room was so stifling.

" . . . I have work to do," she said. "I'd better get on with it." She turned and slipped out of the room.

Thomas called after her as though they were still talking: "Justice couldn't see a thing. But she'd catch a kid every time . . ."

118

No!

"I . . . and name the kid. And never call a wrong name —blindfolded!"

Mrs. Douglass slipped inside Justice's room and closed the door firmly behind her. She leaned against the door, breathing rapidly.

Honestly, he is so devilish, she thought about Thomas. I don't know what he thinks he's trying to do! I mustn't let the boys get the best of me.

Over the years, they'd often pretend to be each other. Parents of identicals had to get used to games like that. She might spend days thinking one was the other. It had been exasperating at times; but the boys had played such tricks less and less as they grew older.

She calmed herself, going over to the bed where Justice lay sound asleep. Justice looked like a rumpled doll. She had the kitchen radio cradled in her arms. It was plugged in behind the bed and the cord was tangled between her toes. Her shoes and socks lay at the foot of the bed where she had kicked them; and she had bunched a woven knapsack beneath her head.

Mrs. Douglass eased away the rough knapsack; Justice's head lolled sideways onto her pillow. Then Mrs. Douglass carefully removed the radio from her arms. Justice woke, eyes half open, and clutched it back again.

"Mom . . . Mommy. You're home." Smiling.

"Shhh . . . Hi, baby. Go back to sleep."

Lightly, Mrs. Douglass kissed Justice, and Justice snuggled in the hollow of her mother's neck.

Her face was hot and wet with perspiration, Mrs. Douglass noticed. Her breath was warm and even. It was so nice having still a baby in the house. Well, not really a baby, Mrs. Douglass thought. But Justice wasn't quite grown-up yet, either. Mrs. Douglass touched her hair. Justice's eyes remained half open and her mother saw sleep enter them again.

"I'm taking the radio away so you can rest," she said softly.

"Don't take it," Justice moaned. She awoke, eyes gazing sleepily at her mom. "It was saying things about Thomas and Levi," Justice said.

Mrs. Douglass laughed. "Over the radio?"

"Oh," Justice said. She had to smile. "Must've been dreaming."

"I guess," said Mrs. Douglass. She eased the radio free and reached across the bed and down over the side to pull out the plug.

"It says a lot about weather," Justice mumbled. "Weather all over the world."

"On this little bitty radio?" Mrs. Douglass said gently.

"All over the States. And a dust bowl is coming."

"It'll rain soon," Mrs. Douglass said. "It always does."

"All over the world," Justice whispered as sleep overtook her, "dust is coming."

Mrs. Douglass regarded her daughter. She held the radio and bunched the plug under her arm as Justice curled in, knees nearly to her chin. Still a baby she was, so soft and safe in the room. Hands and clothes sweaty and marked with dirt of play.

She knew that perhaps she was being sentimental, but lying there she saw sweet innocence showing signs of learning and growing. Of knowing. What more could there possibly be!

Mrs. Douglass was satisfied with what she saw—her little Ticey, exhausted from playing too hard.

120

But at least stay home for the winter quarter, Mrs. Douglass thought. Make sure Ticey eats right. The boys are so busy when school is on. Who will take care of her then? Silently, she left the room, pulling the door to, but not shutting it completely.

I do not like closed doors, Mrs. Douglass was reminded.

She headed back down the hall and ran into Thomas coming out of his and Lee's bedroom. He took the radio, carrying it into the kitchen for her.

"Thanks," she said. "I'll get the groceries." But Levi was ahead of her and Thomas, and already had the groceries in the kitchen.

"The food's going to spoil one day," he said as his mother came in. "You forget all the time to put it away."

"I didn't forget. Had to make my rounds," she said. "Anyway, food can't spoil that fast."

"I-i-inn this *heat* it muh-muh-ight," Thomas said. "Sp-specially mmmeat." He pulled out a family pack of chops, holding it up to show Levi.

"Haven't seen that in a while," Levi said.

"And for good reason," his mother said. "Shouldn't have pork more than once a month."

"We going to have them tonight, I hope?" Levi said.

'Well, we shouldn't," she said. "It's too hot. But I'm hungry for them, I truly am."

"A-a-and some cccorn!" Thomas exclaimed.

"On the cob?" she asked. "I didn't buy any on the cob."

"No, whole-kernel," said Levi, "canned. And we fry it up with bacon and green pepper and onion."

"A-a-and butter," Thomas added.

"Can we have the chops from in the oven?" asked Levi. "Smothered in tomato sauce!"

"Goodness," Mrs. Douglass said.

"A-a-and no-no gr-green veh-veh—greens at-at all," Thomas said. "But bbbaked po-ta-to."

"Yeah!" Levi said.

"That's probably too much starch," Mrs. Douglass said. "Well. I'd better put the potatoes in soon if we're to have them for dinner. First, let me change my clothes. I'll only take a minute. Get out of these slacks into some shorts."

"I'll put the potatoes in," Levi said. "And I'll start the meat." He could cook chops as well as she, Mrs. Douglass knew.

It was so nice to have the boys with her all to herself this way. She appreciated close and simple family things, particularly after a long day away from home.

Levi had the potatoes out and was rinsing them in the sink. She and Thomas finished putting the groceries away.

"Lee," she said, "turn the oven on high for a while. Let the potatoes get started . . ."

"I know," he said.

". . . before you put in the chops. And don't forget to season them first before you put on the sauce. And use the porcelain pan."

"Mom, I *know,*" Levi told her.

"H-h-heee *knows,*" Thomas echoed.

"Okay, guys," she said, "I'll be back in a minute." She smiled brightly at them.

They grinned back, barely, already busy with the feast they would make.

"I'll do the corn when I come back," she said, and left them.

Levi put potatoes in the oven, turning up the heat to 450°.

Thomas stiffened as something seemed to come over him. His eyes turned dark and brooding. A long look passed between him and his brother as Levi closed the oven.

Levi paled. Terror-stricken, he covered his eyes as his brother's gaze on him turned deadly. But then, in a futile gesture, he let his hands fall to his sides.

Thomas' look was harsh and triumphant. Clearly, in less than a minute he had won out about something. And giving Levi one last cold, commanding stare, he lunged for the side door and vanished from the house.

The kitchen became unnaturally quiet as Lee, like a sleepwalker, went over to the counter again. Absent-mindedly, he began slowly seasoning chops and slicing onions.

Outside, just out of sight of the side door, Thomas leaned against the house. He had opened that strange passageway between his brother's mind and his own. Now he funneled himself—his mind—through the passage to stand to one side in his brother's brain. He certainly had perfect control. And standing there with hot sun on his bare back, he would keep control for as long as he wanted.

7

Levi felt a throb of pain over his left eye as he stood there at the kitchen counter. He couldn't think why he should have a headache now when he felt so good fixing— He couldn't recall what he had been doing. He looked down to see pork chops and onions in the porcelain pan; he didn't remember slicing any onions. He did recall having turned the oven up high to cook potatoes. He must have been daydreaming, because he sure didn't recall those onions. And he would have to wait awhile on the potatoes before he could turn down the oven and put the meat in.

Levi poured sauce evenly over the chops. There was something in the back of his mind he needed to remember. He had to tell his mom something important, but each time he tried to remember what it was, his head would throb all the harder.

He thought vaguely, Something to do with Ticey, and his headache immediately got worse.

Or did it have to do with Tom-Tom?

Through a cloud of headache pain, he remembered Thomas disappearing from the house. But that was all.

Mom . . . Warn . . .

Pain exploded behind his eye, halting all thought. Levi sucked air through clenched teeth and stifled a wrenching moan. Now it was revealed to him what was happening. Thomas was inside his brain. He could feel his brother's strength surrounding him. Knew that he was a prisoner and that there was no escape for him until Thomas was finished with him and let him go.

Warn Mom about what, Lee? Thomas stood to one side, tracing these words on Levi's mind. This way of communicating mind within mind pleased him. For while tracing, he never stuttered.

Not so much to warn, finally Levi traced back. He sighed inwardly. Standing at the counter, he was shaking. Thomas had spun an illusion. Levi saw himself trapped in a wooden cup with a crack in it from rim to base. The cup soaked in a dishpan; and through the crack it was filling with soapy water. Thomas could weave terrible illusions. Levi had been forced in the past to visit incredible places where he was in constant danger. Thomas' strength over him weakened his nerve and damaged his will.

Yeah, buddy, you're weak, all right, Thomas traced. *But it's not my fault. I couldn't do any of this if you were ever strong enough to stop me.*

Then why do you have to do it? Levi traced.

Well, do I ever get you hurt? Huh?

You scare me half to death, traced Levi. *Get me out of this cup, will you? The dishwater's up to my knees!*

Don't you think I know it? Thomas traced back. *Don't be such a scaredy-cat, Lee. I get afraid of it the same as you and I'm the one that has to figure a way for you to get out.*

One of these times, I'll never get out. I'll die!

Now, don't be dumb. But Thomas could feel Levi's terror grow as the dishwater rose to his waist. Thomas conjured up some underwater cement and tossed a tube of it over the rim of the cup to Levi.

Levi caught it and quickly began to seal the crack. He

saw handholds and footholds materialize up the side of the cup where there had been none a moment before.

Thanks, Levi traced as he began to climb out.

Sorry I didn't think of it sooner, Thomas traced back.

Levi was over the rim. He jumped down into darkness, full of the sense that his brother was with him and would land him on something dry and soft. He landed on a worn mattress on the floor of a small, cold cell. There were bars all around him. He tested them, but they were strong metal and he could not get out.

What was it you were gonna warn Mom about? Thomas traced.

Let me out of here! And get me rid of this headache, Tom-Tom.

Oh, you'll get out, Thomas traced. *And you'll get over the headache when you tell Mom what I want you to tell her.*

I was just going to tell her about Ticey, Levi traced. *Somehow, but without letting her know what it is Ticey knows. Tom-Tom, why did you have to let Ticey find out about us? It's got her worried and she'll make herself sick with it. And what was the big idea of giving Mom clues like that in the bedroom? You must be clean out of your mind!*

I got my reasons, Thomas traced. *And I'll fix Ticey's wagon, that's the whole point.*

Tom-Tom, you better not hurt her!

That's a laugh, Thomas traced. *Why do you suppose I told Mom stuff like I told her?*

Maybe to cover your tracks, traced Levi, *in case Ticey decides to tell her what she knows.*

Wrong, buddy. And especially I told about Ticey blindfolded . . .

126

That was a lie, too, Levi broke in. *Ticey never cheated and you know it. She was too young even to know how to cheat.*

Boy, Lee, you are what they call some dumb. Ticey never cheated because she didn't have to.

Levi was ever so still in his cell. He clutched the bars until his hands ached, when he began to trace: *You're out of your mind, Tom-Tom.*

Yeah? Then picture this: I couldn't find her out there in the hedgerow this morning—right? Even though I knew she had to be there. But I couldn't find her. Why? Because, buddy, she wouldn't let me find her.

If you think . . . Levi couldn't finish.

You don't have to think anything, dummy, Thomas traced, *because I know. There's not just two of us—you and me. It's you, me and Justice—it's us three!*

Levi bowed his head against the bars and closed his eyes on the darkness. *It's not possible,* he traced weakly, *I would've known. I would have.*

No, not if she didn't know, herself. Don't you see? traced Thomas. *Listen, I didn't get back at her for copying my stutter—you know, when she came back home. Oh, I wasn't going to hurt her. I was planning on scaring her some, make her mad. But I couldn't. And you know why I couldn't? Because they wouldn't let me. But I didn't let them know I knew.*

What? Levi traced. *Didn't let who know you knew what?*

Lee! Don't you get it yet? There ain't only the three of us. There's somebody else. Maybe more than one somebody, and they won't let me break through to Ticey. They have her cut off from us, from me, and keep her from knowing besides.

A moment of stunned silence, after which Levi seemed

to scream through his tracing: *Let me out! I want to get out now—let me out of here, Tom-Tom!*

There was suddenly a huge rumbling in his head, like enormous, echoing steps of a giant.

Listen! Thomas traced. *Mom is coming. And you'd better hear me, too. I'll take away the bars and everything and we'll continue this talk later. But you'll say what I want to Mom. Because I know who has to be keeping me from Justice.*

Maybe you should *be kept from her,* Levi traced quickly. *You just want to hurt her. I know you do!*

Just you remember, Lee. I can give you a headache like nothing you've ever had.

The bars and the cell vanished suddenly as Mrs. Douglass came hurrying into the kitchen. Levi could feel pain from the very top of his head to the bottom of his feet. It was a headache gone on a rampage for a split second as Thomas proved what he could do. Then the pain settled back over Levi's left eye as a throbbing reminder.

"Well!" Mrs. Douglass exclaimed. "I see you have everything ready."

"Just have to open the cans of corn," Levi said easily. All notion of Thomas being present had left him. The memory of their mutual conversation had been folded away in a handkerchief and placed neatly in Thomas' back pocket.

"Don't worry about the corn—I don't need to fix it quite yet," Mrs. Douglass told Levi. "You can put the chops in now, don't you think? Turn down the oven to three-fifty and the potatoes can finish cooking along with the meat."

Levi did as he was told.

"Where did Thomas go?" she asked as he straightened up, closing the oven.

"Oh . . . he ran off somewhere."

"Outside?" she asked.

"I think so. Thomas can't stand much kitchen work," Levi said, and then: "Is Justice still asleep?" He leaned against the counter where he had been working.

"Yes, poor baby, she's exhausted," his mother said. She sat down at the table a moment. Eyes vacant, she sighed, looking tired and somewhat drawn.

Levi wanted to talk to her about how she felt. He wanted to ask if she wasn't doing too much—taking courses and trying to keep up with home, too. He only wanted to sympathize, to show that he cared about her and missed her during the day. But he said nothing. Words would not come to him, as if, when he was about to speak, he would forget even the shape of the words he wanted.

He recalled he had something very important to say. But this, too, escaped him. All that came to mind was something concerning Justice that he didn't really want to speak of. He began saying it, anyway, and he could not stop himself.

"Mom . . ." reluctantly he began. "Justice slips off and kind of roams the whole town—that's why she gets so tired. And I think she's spending a lot of time—maybe too much time—down at Mrs. Jefferson's. I don't know what she does down there. She keeps it secret."

Mrs. Douglass stared at her son. "What do you mean, you don't know what she does? You're supposed to keep an eye on her. You and Thomas both!" She felt anger flare.

Levi stood there, tongue-tied.

"You're supposed to tell her to come home at a certain time," she said. "You don't let her run around at will, she's too young."

"We keep an eye on her, me and Thomas both," Levi said. "I thought you knew she went over to Mrs. Jefferson's.

That's why I never mentioned it."

"Well." She stood, absently rubbing her shoulders. "No, I didn't know that," she said. "Leona's a bit different, keeping to herself the way she does."

"Not just different," Levi said. "The kids all think she's kinda crazy, like a fortune-teller, or something. Thomas thinks so, too."

"Does he, now?" she said. She eyed Levi as he turned, shifted his weight until he had turned his profile to her. "And what do *you* think?" she asked him.

"Me . . . Me?" he said.

"Please look at me when I'm talking to you," she said.

Again he shifted against the counter, facing her. Then he stood straight, as was Levi's formal way.

"I asked you what you thought about Justice visiting Mrs. Jefferson."

"Oh, yeah," Levi said. "Nothing. I mean," he said, "I didn't think anything about it because I thought you knew she went down there."

"Well," she said again, "for your information and for Thomas', I didn't know, but I don't believe there's anything wrong with her visiting Mrs. Jefferson. We had a conversation, Ticey and I did, about difference not too long ago." She gave Levi a searching look. "We talked about you boys, how you are so much alike but also so different."

Levi ran his hand across his forehead, closing his eyes and frowning as he did so.

"Your head hurts you?" Mrs. Douglass asked.

"A little bit. Around my left eye. When I get a headache, it's usually a pain in my left eye."

"That sounds like sinus," she said. "Or maybe we should have your eyes tested."

"Aw, it's probably nothing. It comes and goes." The pain seared him, exploding behind his eye. Levi had one thought. He must try to make his mother stop Ticey from visiting Mrs. Jefferson.

He began, "If Dorian's mom *is* some kind of fortune-teller, maybe she will influence Ticey with all that what's-your-sign stuff and palm-reading. Ticey is awful young. She might take it all to heart and give herself nightmares."

"Oh, now, she's a very down-to-earth child," Mrs. Douglass said firmly. "I'm sure she visits Leona because I'm not around. So she takes the next best mom she can find." She paused, feeling a twinge of guilt. "I'll talk to Ticey, but I'm sure it's all right. Leona may be different, but she's *not* crazy, Tom-Tom."

Calling Levi, Tom-Tom. It was a slip of the tongue, the harmless way a parent will forget and call one of her children by the other's name.

But Levi's face went pale with shock when his mother called him Tom-Tom. For an instant, his eyes ran with fear.

"Lee, I mean," Mrs. Douglass corrected herself. Her voice trailed off as the smugness of Thomas appeared in Lee's expression.

Mrs. Douglass' mouth gaped open. "Thomas!" she whispered.

"What? . . . Mom?" Levi said. A calm and relaxed set to his face, which now showed concern. "Mom?" With a questioning smile, he said, "Just then you called me Thomas."

"Well, for a moment I thought . . . I was sure I saw—"

"Oooh. Ouch!" Levi clutched his brow in an exaggerated show of pain. "Do we have any aspirin? Maybe I do have some sinus."

At once, his mom was full of sympathy. "I don't wonder, with all of the dryness and heat day after day—all of the pollen, the ragweed growing like trees. Maybe it's hay fever. Did you wake up with it?" She went to a cupboard for aspirin.

"Yes. It could be that I slept too hard," he said.

"You boys stay up too late. I've been lax about that. Why is it that, soon as summer comes, the rules fly out the window?"

"We have to have some fun," Levi told her. "We don't go hanging around the streets—aren't you glad of that?"

"But you do smoke cigarettes right in this house, don't you?" She had caught him by surprise. He hung his head.

"I want it stopped," she told him. "Now that you've tried it, you can quit it, okay?"

"Okay," he said quietly.

"And tell Thomas. I'm not going to make a big thing out of it and tell your father, but I want it stopped. Next thing you know, Ticey will be trying it."

"Okay," he said again.

There wasn't much talking between them after that. Levi swallowed milk with his aspirin. He prepared the table for the evening meal in the dining room, where they always had supper. When he finished, he was free to slip back to his room. Gently, he closed the door behind him.

Thomas took the handkerchief from his back pocket. He let memory free.

You did pretty good, he told Levi.

Thanks, traced Levi glumly. Once again, he was aware of bars surrounding him and the dank odor of his tiny cell. *Let me out now, please.*

Just hold on, Thomas traced. *You didn't do all that well.*

You didn't get Mom to come down hard on Ticey for going over to the Jeffersons'.

It's not my fault Mom didn't see anything wrong with her going over there. She said—.

I know what she said, Thomas traced. *I happened to be listening. And you'll stay right where you are for not being more convincing.*

Levi gripped the bars with all of his might. *It's only an illusion,* he told himself. *There aren't any bars. Thomas is just making it up.*

But there *were* bars, that was the horror of it. He could actually see and feel them. There *was* a cell. Levi was of so little strength he could not break out of Thomas' imagination. He bowed his head, feeling desperately alone.

Somewhere there was a sound. Out there, beyond the bars where Thomas' murky presence waited and tormented Levi, the slightest of flutterings. It was a gentle, delicate movement coming to rest, and it was watching.

What—? said Thomas. Levi could sense him searching the dark. *Who's there!*

Levi blinked out into the deep shadows beyond the cell. He saw nothing, but he felt a watching; there was no other way to describe it. Whatever it was was not possible, coming as it did from out of nowhere rather than from Thomas. And he had the impression that Thomas was terrified by it.

Thomas crouched, shielding his head. *Oooh, get away!* Whatever watched made him feel uncomfortably warm. Soon, he was burning hot and he could feel his skin tanning, burning, right there in the darkness of Levi's mind.

Levi could hear Thomas yelling at whatever was watching. Then the bars he held on to dissolved. His tiny cell

133

melted away. Levi stood quaking as the image of himself quaking dwindled.

I'm free!

He found himself on that utterly strange voyage through the narrow, empty passage between Thomas' self and his own. In the passage, his mind was timeless, flowing through a stream of bright nothing. At the last moment, he pulled back in shock. It was Thomas' mind flowing away, not his own. But he had almost mixed his own with his brother's!

Levi came to himself in his room. He had his own mind and he laughed hysterically, his breath exploding in great surges of relief. He grabbed his arms, felt his face, to make certain he was really he and in control of himself. He hugged himself, rocking slowly from side to side.

He fell to trembling, suddenly, remembering how terrible his brother had been to him. Yet he was free for the moment. What had freed him? he wondered. What had been there, so powerful in its watching?

But he knew beyond a doubt that he was trapped forever at Thomas' mercy.

Justice lay deep asleep. No longer was she curled in a ball like a soft, sweet kitten. She lay stiff and unnaturally still. Not a breath appeared to escape her lips. Her hands were knotted into fists and her arms were like petrified sticks crossed over her chest.

Minutes ago, her eyes had come wide open. There was no telling whether she was alert behind them, for they held nothing of her feeling or expression. But there was something ever so clear shining watchful from them.

Behind her open eyes, she lay dreaming. She observed through space and unimaginable places. She saw from the

134

kitchen to Thomas' and Levi's room; then outside, where Thomas now crouched on that side of the house near the room.

Thomas tried to hide himself from what his senses recognized as something alert and watching in the sunlight. He felt it probe at him and deftly warn him that he could not hide.

The Watcher took its time retreating. It faded, finally, and Justice's dreaming submitted to the dark. Her eyes fluttered closed; her body relaxed all at once. So powerful was the loosening of muscles at the same time that she awakened with a start. She stretched, yawned, staring around her. Again she curled comfortably about herself, unwilling to give up her ease for at least another half-hour.

Justice wouldn't wake up again until her mother called her to supper. She was at rest, with nothing on her mind.

8

"You seen him?"

"No, I haven't seen him."

"You seen Tom-Tom?"

"I wasn't even lookin' for him!"

"Yes, you were!"

"No, I wasn't! Maybe he's already gone."

"He hasn't gone, I would of seen him."

"Maybe he left before you were up and out here."

"I been out here since six-thirty!"

"Awwh, you haven't either!"

It was Friday morning. And Thursday evening they none of them had gone to the field after supper. They'd known that Tom-Tom wouldn't want them to. So they had gone to bed early in order to get a good start on Friday.

Since seven, boys had been shooting out of driveways and plunging up and down Dayton Street on their bikes, past the Union Road.

"I think he's already gone. I haven't seen a soul from up there all morning."

"Maybe because it's too early for them to be up, dummy."

"I think I saw Mr. Douglass go."

"You think."

"I know I saw him, around six-thirty."

"I think I saw him, too. Yeah. I know I did. Had to be him."

136

"But nobody else's come out."

"Think we oughta go up and check?"

"Up the field?"

"Around Union, on our bikes. Just ride up the driveway and see if *their* bikes—"

"Awm not goin' up there."

"Why not?"

"S'bad enough goin' up the field."

"What er you talking about!"

"You know. They're twins and all."

"They're identicals, my mom says Mrs. Douglass says is better than calling them twins. Because nothing they do is the same thing. Twins is a non-word, my mom says Mrs. Douglass says. Says what they are is identicals. Anyway, I've known them for as long as they been here."

"Me, too."

"And they're just like anybody. One's smart in books and the other is smart-ass, my mom and dad says."

Laughter from the boys. Snickering.

"Well, they do!"

"We believe you. We believe you!"

"Tom-Tom ain't dumb."

"Well, I know that. He ain't smart, either."

"But he can sure play those drums."

"Bet he can play anything—hey, you remember the time they let us try all the horns and things to see if we wanted to play anything? You remember Tom-Tom picking them up and playing them? I mean, playing them like he'd been practicing them. The teacher said, 'Tom Douglass, who's your private teacher?' And Tom-Tom just shook his head."

"I don't remember nothing like that, and I was there."

"Well, it's true, I was there, too!"

"I believe you. I believe you. Calm down! You want folks to notice what we are doing?"

There were an unusual number of boys and bikes riding around at such an early hour. Folks hurrying off to work didn't pay much attention. It was summer and kids were going to be around the streets. It would be two months before even the boys thought about school and the long snow-time of winter.

"You think he's taken off on us just to get the best snakes first?"

"I know one way to find out."

The three worriers spun out of the group at the corner of Union and Dayton. In sixty seconds, they had sped clear across town and over the treacherous Morrey route to race down the Quinella Road. They made it, oblivious to traffic in this early morning.

The boys rode expertly down. In no time, they were in the field beside the road, running through high weeds and searching along the black waters of the Quinella Trace. They did not find Tom-Tom.

"What am I doing out here?"

"It was your idea."

"Because you said he was down here."

"I never said he was down here!"

"Yes, you did, too!"

"No, I said he was *maybe* down here."

"You said he was down here. And like a fool, I listened. Man, I bet he ain't even up yet."

They were in a sweat now. One of them noticed that, although sunny up above, the day was swathed in ground fog down here. Misty, it was damp, like the tropics, with steam trapped under the great shade trees.

"Let's get on outta here."

138

"Let me catch my breath."

"Stay down here, standing still too long and you catch some snakebite."

"And without Tom-Tom around to take care of it."

"Sure. Now he can fix a snakebite."

"Sure. I know a kid in Eighth Grade says he was bit down here by something big and long. It wasn't any kind of garter snake, neither. And Tom-Tom come along, says, 'Let me see where you was bit.' And the kid shows him. There it was on the leg, you could see the puncture marks, so the kid said. Tom-Tom looks at the bite real queer for a long look. Then he drops the kid's pants leg and says, 'Why, look at all them crows up the tree!' The kid goes and looks at the crows. He says there was a whole lot of them, real funny the way they was all there in one tree. When he turns back again, Tom-Tom is way off, running away. Looking back over his shoulder at the kid. The kid heads on home from there and doesn't think about the snakebite until he's about halfway up the Quinella Road. He remembers he was bit. 'I was bit! Oh, me, am I gunna die? I was *bit!*' And falls off his bike, and sits down right there on the side of the road. And starts cryin', too scared yet to roll up his pants leg again and look at the bite. He's sure he's dying, and he's heaving and blubbering and feels faint because he'd been pedalin' the bike so hard and it's real hot out; but he don't think of that for a reason at all."

"I can feel like fainting any time coming up that hill on a hot day."

"Me, too."

"So he's sittin' there, bawling like a baby and a good thing it's the middle of the day and no cars. Somebody'd sure see him and go back and tell his folks."

"Ain't it funny how someone you know always sees ya

139

when ya don't want even a stranger to see ya?"

"Because you are doin' what you have no business."

"So a half-hour passes. The kid can breathe easier and he stops his crying. He ain't dead yet. And he gets up his courage. He rolls up his pants leg real slow and careful, like he's rolling up a million dollars in tens—either of you ever own a ten?"

The two stay quiet a moment. Glumly, one looks away.

Finally, the other says, "When I had me a paper route. This guy comes out with an arm in a sling and digging in his jeans to pay me for the month. He pulls out this bill. I take it. I think it's a one. He says, 'You got change for that?' I look at it and it's a ten. 'Nope,' I says back at him. I'm holding that ten and feeling how it feels in muh hand. Then I get this strong whiff of the dude. Man, he's drunk! And near out of it. And the bandages look brand new, like he ran into a tree only an hour ago, or just a little while ago rolled down the front steps. Anyway. He can't keep his eyes steady good. So I says real careful, 'Mister, I ain't got the change.' And he says, 'Well, what in hell I owe ya?' And I says, pulling out my book—and before I can even say, he says, 'Seven-fifty, wunnit?' My mouth falls open, but I clamp it shut again real fast. And I don't say nothing. And he says, 'Well, hell, I ain't got nothin' smaller, so keep the change.' And I kept it all. Got me a sweet ol' ten-dollar bill."

They are silent. The one that is the leader of the three moves away from the Quinella Trace back across the open field of high weeds. The other two follow, and mist encloses all of them and trails behind them as they hurry though the gray air.

The leader speaks. "This kid I was talking about finishes rolling up his pants leg. He must've rolled up the wrong one because there ain't a mark on his right leg, which he was sure was the one was bit. So, quick this time, he rolls up the left leg, taking it easy and careful when he gets near where he thinks the bite is. But there ain't a bite on that leg, either. He stares at both legs, and whatever was there sure ain't there anymore. And he looks hard. But not even a twinge."

"Ahwh!" The two boys laugh. The leader is proud at how good the story still sounds. Proud that he didn't forget any of it; it's not the easiest thing for him to tell something with no mistake all the way through. He believes the story without going deeper. Not to say that he believes Tom-Tom can heal a snakebite wound. But he tells the story because Tom-Tom is in it and he enjoys the sound of the telling.

They reclaim their bikes beside the road and head back up the winding Quinella.

"Once I seen Tom-Tom and his brother—" one of them says.

"Lee," the leader tells him.

"No, but that's not his whole name."

"Levi," the third one says promptly.

"Yeah. I see him and Levi coming home from school. Levi's arms were full of books. He carried everything for his brother, including that plastic water bottle all them soccer players use. And before Tom-Tom gave up most all sports for drumming.

"Anyhow, Tom-Tom is walking along, headin' the soccer ball—you know, knocking it around with his head. . . ."

"We know. We know," the leader says. They are riding three in a row across the road. They try to keep their minds on the story, ride with style and listen for cars coming up from behind at the same time.

Style loses.

"Well, it was funny, is all I'm talking about."

"What was funny?" the leader says. "What happened?"

"Nothin' *happened*. What it was, I couldn't see that they were talking to each other. Tom-Tom was in front of Levi. And every time Tom-Tom would grin, Levi would nod behind him. Or one of them would shake his head and the other would frown right back. One did something and the other did something that fit with what the first had done."

He looked at the other two for approval, for confirmation. Vaguely, he was aware that he hadn't made himself clear. He hadn't thought far enough, perhaps because what he wished to say was not yet clear to him.

The two who had been listening made no comment. All three raced over the B&O tracks to the top of the hill and on across town. Once in the neighborhood, they found the rest of the boys scattered away from the corner of Dayton and Union. So they took a route along a side street to be less conspicuous, and came out again at the far end of Dayton. Seeing them, the rest of the boys began gathering. All were still waiting long after the last of the parents on Dayton Street had gone to work. Every mom and dad had driven off, except for Dorian Jefferson's mom, Mrs. Leona Bethune Jefferson, and his dad, Mr. Buford Jefferson. She was the only one now at home all day. It used to be that Tom-Tom's and Levi's mom was home all day, too, but not now. She had driven off like the others—but she was late, as usual.

It felt to the boys like it took all day for nine o'clock to come and go. By nine-fifteen, they were racing around on their bikes and unsettling dust the length of the street. The clear sunlight of early morning had gathered above them like a misty brown stain of pollution. Heat was oppressive, and boys were dripping sweat around their necks and hairlines. Every boy in Justice's Pickle and Cream Gang had made it home at least once, using the house keys tied safely on cords now dripping wet around their necks. They were silent, entering homes left mussed and dish-strewn from the morning's rush. They could always find something to eat—dry cereal eaten directly from the carton, or a piece of bread, toast with jam. They found jars full of sugarless gum and stuffed their pockets with it.

One had thrown down his key on its cord the moment he came into the kitchen. Slick, the leader of the three who had been on the early-morning run down the Quinella Road looking for Tom-Tom by the river. Now he finished a can of cream soda while standing in the light of the open refrigerator door. He swallowed the pop and it hit him that he had to catch a bunch of snakes, enough to fill up his peanut-butter container—cram it as full as he could get it. A lot of little snakes were needed. It gave him the creeps to think about it. He concentrated on the sticky-sweet soda. At last, he closed the refrigerator, which had cooled him off some.

The house was creepy, though, with just him in it—the reason why each day he stayed in the streets. Or maybe three or four of them would go fool around at the community center, but they got bored with pool. And fooling around, they were liable to miss whatever went on in the neighborhood. Who knew when Tom-Tom was going to call them to the field? Without question, without a thought, he knew that Tom-Tom was not the same as the rest of them.

He smoothed down his hair and thought to wash his face and neck under the kitchen faucet. His face stung him as water hit under the eyes. The skin over his cheekbones was raw from sunburn. He dried off in a hurry and forgot to pick up his house key from the counter. And with the race on his mind, he slammed out of the house, locking himself out for the whole day.

It might have been hours later, the boys down at the far end of the street were so worn out from waiting. Yet it was only ten o'clock. Where there had been an empty corner at Union and Dayton a moment ago, there now swung into view three figures. Their well-kept bikes made the thinnest, sleekest sound of perfect working order in the suddenly silent street. Pausing, they swung onto Dayton and away toward Tyler, where the smallest figure broke formation and executed a lazy, no-hands figure-eight in the middle of the street.

"Lookit that Justice!" one of the boys said loud. "She has to be in on everything!"

Justice gave them a wave of her arm before tearing back after her brothers. She took her place alongside the one they'd seen had a bunch of things, yellow containers, slung up his arm. There was no mistaking Levi, anyway. Although he rode the same kind of bike as Thomas'—a black, high-seated racer—he rode with his shoulders hunched too high; his head bowed too low, as though worry made it too heavy to bear.

Suddenly, the boys, close to ten of them, raced out from the far end of Dayton Street.

"They're going to be outta sight," one of them yelled, "and we're sitting here!"

Just as Dorian Jefferson tore down the steps of his house. He wore a once white T-shirt now old and faded pink. He was barefoot, with brown overalls cut off, curiously, just below his knees. They noticed his legs were pockmarked with mosquito and chigger bites. Falling over himself into the street, he grinned from ear to ear and leaped on the back of the nearest bike as it was passing. The bike wavered, zigzagged, before it steadied.

"Man, Dorian," yelled Slick Peru, "why me?" And then: "Fool, where're your shoes?"

On cue, Dorian's shoes came sailing out of the house, hitting the shoulders of a couple of boys. All of them had stopped by now and had come over to group their bikes in front of Dorian's house. They caught a glimpse of Mrs. Jefferson as she slipped back inside. Something in the way she paused, holding the door open before she went in— they hadn't seen her face. Her hair wasn't combed; she still wore a dark robe. But they knew she hadn't thrown his shoes outside in anger. They noticed her, realized once again that they were responsible for Dorian, and forgot her.

"Dorian, man!" Slick said again, Dorian wasn't quite grinning. He had jumped off of Slick's bike and now sat in the street struggling to get knots out of his frayed shoelaces. One of the fellows leaned over, grabbed up the other shoe and quickly untied it. Handing it to Dorian, he took the other shoe out of Dorian's hand and untied it while Dorian worked to put on the first shoe.

The three figures had come back into view at the other end of the street.

"We almost ready," Dorian called to them.

Justice had a mind to go down and see what was going on. Her view was of bikes and a pack of boys in a bunch, when she divined it was Dorian in there on the ground, putting his shoes on.

Knowing Thomas and Levi were next to her. Inwardly, she was suddenly aware of a delicate but foreign touch along her thoughts. It was not the same as the friendly, shining observer that lately she would imagine came to her just as she awoke or went to sleep. But this remote touching was like someone hiding from her and listening in on her mind. She had lately recognized for a few minutes at a time that it was a presence among her thoughts; and she understood that it had been with her over a long period of time, perhaps even years. She understood for a few seconds that Mrs. Jefferson erected shields to protect Justice as best she could from the presence, and to keep her from understanding too much too quickly of the bright watching. No sooner did Justice have this clarity than it began to fade.

Wait!

Awkwardly, she reached with something that felt like a flow of electric current. Its sparkling essence surprised and thrilled her. And with it, she was able to pull her mind away from the presence trying to read her.

You, Thomas. She was careful to trace this only to herself.

Cautiously, she skirted the looming presence, which was unable to disguise itself as anything other than an outsider and an intruder.

There!

Abruptly, all ultra-sensory turned off for her, as if a vast, shining window had its dark shade pulled down. Swiftly, Justice lost completely the ability to see inwardly and had no knowledge that she ever could. She was unaware of the moment when Thomas left off his scan of her thoughts. But he had, a second or so after her ability ceased. He had emptied out of her mind and sat there on his bike with a grim expression on his face. Once again, he'd found noth-

146

ing; yet he knew there was much there to discover beyond Justice's unresolved impressions, which was about all he ever found.

"You-youuuu *guys!*" His voice burst down the street. All of the boys down there hushed and sat still.

"G-g-ge-ehht in l-*line!*"

The boys raced up the street on their bikes and grouped around Thomas, Levi and Justice.

Thomas and Levi exchanged thoughtful, identical looks. Right afterward, Levi began explaining things:

"You guys could of gone down to the Quinella any time before ten. You could of had your snakes already back here. Now we're running late and going to look conspicuous."

"What's that mean?" someone whispered.

"Attract attention," was the loud whisper back.

They all listened, somehow knowing it was Thomas making himself clear through his brother.

"You're to ride in twos," Levi told them, "and keep to the side. Now we have to worry about cops noticing us and wondering what we're doing."

The boys looked upset that they had started out wrong. Most of them were still eager to please. But one or two looked belligerently at Levi. That passed quickly when they caught Thomas watching them.

"C-c-come *on!*" He wheeled his racer around in a cloud of dust and was fifteen yards away before any of them had made a move.

Justice and Levi were the first to react. They started up, getting the boys in formation as they went. There were eleven kids counting all, including themselves, and ten bikes. With Thomas gone ahead, it worked out even when Slick and his rider were centered alone behind Justice and

Levi. Thomas in front and Justice and Levi riding behind him. Third came the single bike of Slick's with Dorian hanging on the back. After them, the rest of the boys came on in twos to make it even at the end.

They sped across town, hugging close to the right side of the road. They were some out-of-town contingent in search of the local parade. But there weren't a great many people at this hour around to see them. People were at work and sidewalks were empty. There wasn't a police cruiser anywhere in sight as they came to the light at Xenia Avenue on its green signal. Without an iota of caution, they all saw Thomas streak through. They followed at breakneck speed.

The Quinella Road! She felt the air puff her hair like the bulging of a sail. Gathering such speed on the downward Quinella, they all did, that she created wind along the path of her rush-through.

I am flat-out and flying!

Levi with her, and the rest of the boys right behind them. But no bike could overtake Thomas on his. How could it be when they both had the same bikes—his and Levi's—that his was fastest?

He had a head start, Thomas did. But his is always fastest anyway.

Justice was herself coasting dangerously fast on the downward road. Smack in front of a whole pack a *boys!* she thought. All of them older'n me. And with my brothers, on the way to making The Great Snake Race.

Thoughts sang on the wind in her ears.

How do I slow down everybody, she wondered, so they can see me perform?

Justice had pictured it differently. She had imagined

herself as somehow on high, doing her bike trick to perfection. The boys would be in a circle, looking up at her and wildly applauding when she had finished.

Now she knew better.

Break formation and I'll cause the worst accident anybody's ever seen.

She had a vivid picture of boys, unable to stop, crashing into one another. Bent wheels and tires going flat. Broken bones and blood!

She tasted disappointment. She was about to give up all hope of performing the trick she'd practiced all week when it came to her how it could be done.

She speeded up and cut fast diagonally, away from Levi, to the right side of the road. She was going down at really fast speed when she began to squeeze the brakes ever so gently. She was way to the side and out of the way of oncoming bikes. Startled boys gave her questioning looks as they raced by her. They didn't break formation.

She had a fleeting glimpse of Levi straining to see where she'd gone to before he was engulfed by the armada.

"Justice!" she heard him calling.

"I'm coming last!" Yelling as loud as she could. It was not loud enough. She heard boys shouting to Levi: "She's going to come up last, she says."

"What for!" Levi again.

"She didn't say!" Boys answering.

Justice brought up the rear, careful to keep her distance but not so far back that she would lose sight of them on the other side of a hill. She speeded again, with her mind on having the boys pass the flat place in the road and on to the fence just when she reached the flat place. Thomas would be furious at her for breaking formation and would probably say, "Justice, whater you doing?" He would stutter it—something like that, anyway. And then she would perform her trick, with all eyes watching. They, none of them, would expect it to be so expert and professional. Levi would probably say she was a true artist, she knew he would. And the boys would stare at her like they'd never seen her before.

Wind was in her hair, pressing in her face. She talked to herself in it. She felt it like a veil of coolness. She heard herself laughing, only it was the way she might sound when she was older. Then she quit laughing and talking to herself. She concentrated on the last hill and over, and the downward coast. Oh, it was so fast!

Spread out below were all of the boys, with Thomas, way in front, turned in the road to wait for them. But he seemed to be looking beyond the boys toward Justice coming down the last unbelievably fast hill.

She released the handlebars and folded her arms across her chest. At such speed, she had to hold her feet exactly even, rock-still on the pedals all the while, steering with the lower half or her body. She was leaning slightly forward, but remained rigid, sort of a post, leaning. She was in complete control and kept her sight on that flat, empty place in the road where she would perform. It was coming on fast.

The bike armada had passed the place in the road and was gathering where Thomas waited in front of the fence at the field. As Thomas went on staring beyond the boys, they turned in unison to see. They all watched, puzzled, as Justice sped down.

All this happening in the green, dusty stillness of country in seconds; and Justice knowing they were all watching. She saw boys suddenly pull their bikes off the road. Did

150

they think she would perform right in front of them and not in the flat place just above them? Actually, the place was a slight hollow or depression in the general incline of this part of the Quinella Road before it became flat and uneventful.

Justice was nearly there.

Ready!

She gave a careless glance to the side, reasonably certain that nothing was coming down the hill. She thrilled to see the empty, forward road. Nothing, not one car coming on. She saw boys jerking their arms to the left, telling her to get out of the road. She was intent on her performance and paid them no mind.

The wind was in her hearing; it grew loud.

Set!

Down at the base of the hill, there was less of an incline. She definitely lost speed. Grasping the seat beneath her, she took her feet off the pedals. She stretched her legs stiffly up and forward until they rested on the handlebars.

Boys were yelling at her. She thought to smile for them. Levi looked stricken, his mouth open.

Don't worry, Levi!

Thomas was walking back toward the boys. His face looked startled, staring at Justice—no, she noticed, he was looking beyond her.

She was in her graceful couch pose, ready to make the slight lean that would start her bike turning in clean circles. About to let herself Go! and be Spectacular Justice, to loom in the minds of her brothers and the other boys as better than The Great Snake Race. She was holding herself so tight together, and yet so relaxed. Her heart beat fast and steady against her chest.

A horn, blasting, split her eardrums. The sound of it tore

through her, blaring and bending its tone in a mournful wail. She lost her balance. Speeding away, the car blasted her dream.

Justice spun off the bike and toppled on her side. Her own momentum swept her over onto her hands and knees. Her riderless bike sailed on past the boys and Thomas. It hit something at the edge of the road. It lifted and plunged into high grass, leaping toward the fence, where it stopped on impact and fell over.

Somebody had her under the arms. Her hands were stinging and throbbing. Her knees felt like they had holes of pain. She must look like an idiot, she thought.

Levi lifted her up.

"Oooh . . . ooow . . . " There were shivers of pain in her legs and down her side.

"Justice, are you okay? Are you hurt?"

She limped around, shaking her head to let Levi know she wasn't hurt badly. But she *was* hurt. She imagined blood where a knee was scraped, it hurt so, and refused to look again. She kept her face turned away from the boys, standing quietly with their bikes.

"Honest, I thought you were going to get killed. What were you trying to do?" Levi asked her.

"Wait till I get my bike and I'll show you," she said, her voice unsteady. She was still stunned and shaken from the sudden, screaming blast of the car horn.

"Look," Levi said, his voice low so the others wouldn't hear, "I told you to stick with me. Now, I mean it! No more tricks—was it a trick you were trying to do? Do you want Tom-Tom to get started on you and me, too?"

She was silent. The last thing she wanted was to cause Levi some trouble. She covered her palms with her fingers.

152

The palms were bruised and tender, hurting enough to make tears come to her eyes. She imagined her knees had deep gashes running with blood that was seeping dark and wet through her jeans. She flexed her knees. They hurt and were probably bruised.

"Come on," Levi said to her, whispering. She divined by the whisper that Thomas was watching and waiting.

When she turned to face the field, she saw him standing at the flat of the road, one hand on his hip and the other holding her bike by the seat.

Slowly, she went over to him. She didn't want to look at the boys, all watching, and she didn't want to meet Thomas' gaze. Never mind Thomas. He wasn't even looking at her, but at a point on the hill above her. He let his gaze travel up and over the hill and beyond.

Telling her to go home, she was sure of it, and she lost her courage to be the only girl to keep up with them. Ashamed of herself, she reached for the bike. Thomas let go of it before they would be holding it at the same time.

So mean!

She caught the bike as he turned away. He never said a word to her.

"The dumb car," she told him, only for him to hear. "I had this trick—"

It was no use talking. He was headed for the boys. Swaggering away from her, he was smart to ignore her. Smart not to talk and stutter, which would have weakened the effect of him as their commander.

The boys laid their bikes down in the same formation, next to the fence, as Thomas gestured to them to follow him. They slipped through the fence and on into the high weeds toward the Quinella Trace. Dorian half turned, seeking out Justice, his expression respectful, kind. Justice hung her head and Dorian went on with the rest.

Levi headed for the fence. He paused, turning to her. "You sure you're going to be all right?"

"Yeah," she said.

"Well, if you want to come, come on," he said resignedly. And then: "Nobody else had to do a trick and risk hurting themselves and everybody else, too. Can't you let him have his day?" Meaning Thomas. "Don't try so hard. You're with us, it's okay. And don't cause any more trouble."

Gingerly, he eased his way through the barbed wire while she stood, huddled and small, holding her bike. She knew so much about Levi. Knew he didn't care about The Great Snake Race the way Thomas did. Probably if it had been up to him, he would have stayed home. But, for some reason, he had to be around when Thomas commanded the boys. Or maybe—yes—he had to keep an eye on Thomas for some reason.

Justice's legs trembled from the exertion. She felt slightly sick to her stomach.

Even Levi, she thought. He'd rather I stayed home. I always try too hard.

For an instant, she had a desperate feeling of being abandoned, as though she were lost forever from all that was dear to her.

From Mom and Dad, too?

From your mom and dad as well.

Some part of her mind seemed to answer. It stood separately, in order to survive after she was lost.

Justice's eyes welled with tears; a lump ached in her throat. Somewhere inside herself, she was small and deserted, with the day grown strange, and huge with mist around her.

154

But the dismal sensation disappeared as mysteriously as it had come. Justice heard sounds of the day again. Trees along the road, some slight sound of branches and leaves in a faint flutter of motion. She heard boys along the Quinella Trace and she could see some of them over there.

Best to go home, I guess.

Yet it didn't surprise her that she calmly took her bike over and put it in formation with the others, right next to Levi's. She laid the bike on its side, letting it touch Levi's.

If you're staying, get on in the field.

She went through the fence and into the weeds which felt steamy and smelled of wet rot.

This is not a good day.

She stayed away from the boys along the river, whom she saw bending and straightening as they rushed around. Justice stayed on the far side, with the great shade trees between her and the boys at the Trace.

Means to follow lines, she thought. Trace.

She followed an invisible line in the lonesome mist on the far side of the trees. The boys would find it difficult to see her there unless they were looking hard. Moving cautiously, she kept her eyes on the ground and gathered herself inward. Justice was certain she left only a slight trace of herself.

Knowing she must walk among snakes and begin her hunt. She came out of the trees just before the place where the Quinella Trace made a bend to the west. It had been parallel to the Quinella Road and was now perpendicular to it. It flowed away into the distance of land reaches, weeds and thick undergrowth. It definitely became less of a river and more a clogged stream full of crawdaddies and mosquitoes. Justice wouldn't follow it that far. She came out into the area between the deep shade of the trees and the

Trace, just below the river bend.

Snake beds all around, she felt numbed, less aware of boys close at hand. Snakes quivered and scurried if she moved at all quickly. By standing still for seconds on end, then carefully moving and standing still again, she could come quite near writhing clumps, as she had on her first snake hunt.

Justice saw thin, young-looking snakes, all intertwined. Boys were grabbing snakes whenever creatures loosed themselves a bit from the clumps. She saw boys, even Levi, stuffing snakes into peanut-butter buckets.

They're dumb to race so many. How will they know which belongs to who? Tie colored ribbons on their tails?

She saw Thomas coming near. His yellow container was full of dark creatures moving within. She headed in the opposite direction so as not to get in his way. Passing the bend in the river, she searched the flat, dry shore and the space in between.

It dawned on her how unusual, how weird was the Trace. In a rush of feeling, she divined the beginning, the primal urge which caused these ordinary snakes from the surrounding land to return again and again to this home of their ancient past. To mate and bear their young.

There is this trace of the long gone and dead. Maybe they follow the trails, the scent of awful heat and terrible ice cold. Of living and dying. And changing! she thought. And unable to hear, and no eyelids, no arms or legs. Crawling, slithering, the lowest life of all.

She felt a sudden sympathy: You creatures.

She felt joy: Hugging the ground. Finding holes and cracks deep down. You stay warm. You live. And never die out.

9

Justice was staring at a large tree limb where it lay decaying, dark and moist, near the Quinella water. Absently, she scratched at her ankles, where chiggers or mites had found their way to her skin and buried themselves in it. It was only a fallen branch she kept her eye on, perhaps struck by lightning. And it was the contour, the outline of the wood along its upper surface, that had caught her eye. As she stared, the wood separated along its top contour, fairly jumping at her. Lying there was a big, beautiful garter, the fattest and longest she'd seen. Its camouflage of dark lines and lengthwise stripes hadn't been good enough for Justice's keen sight.

She sucked in her breath. At once, she covered her mouth to hush the sound. Of course, she knew snakes couldn't hear; it had been a natural reaction. She kept herself from rushing forward, knowing that the snake might feel the vibration of her steps.

Justice saw movement out of the corner of her eye, coming up on her left from the direction of the river bend. Without turning or seeing for certain which one of the boys it would have to be, she held up her hand flat against the air to warn him to stand still. And pointing at the rotting log, she showed him the snake. Then she waited, still as a statue. And the boy, whoever he was, was a solid presence at the edge of her vision.

Until the natural solitude of river sounds, of branches that reached low, begging for water, settled down on them. Until the dry, caked dust of the bank crawled with water creatures—striders, and huge bugs that seemed ugliest of all to Justice. And there were snakes: sleek, dark water snakes, but no moccasins; and the ribbon snake, small and young, newly born. It looked like a garter except that its stripes were bright yellow on a dark form.

Justice hadn't noticed the few boys who spied the scene from a distance. They came forward now, tiptoeing up behind Thomas, who was the boy she hadn't quite seen out of the corner of her eye. Thomas rolled his eyes skyward. He pointed at Justice and then at the snake. The boys made exaggerated mouthings of "Wha—?" "You kidding?" "That big snake? What for?"

Squinting at Justice, Thomas pointed his finger at his own head and made a circle at his temple. Putting a finger to his lips, he next signaled the boys to stay quiet. He waved them bye-bye. They nodded, grinning, and left.

Silently, one foot in front of the other, Justice moved up on the snake. She hoped it wouldn't sense her and slither away into the water.

You go slow enough and it won't know, she thought.

She could feel her pulse in her temples. Heat pressed in on her bare arms.

Just a little coolness is all I want.

All at once, she felt that the hot air she breathed would smother her.

Stop it. Stop it. You'd think the clouds would cool it some. Why won't there be clouds anymore?

Justice stood still a moment to calm herself. Without her knowing, Thomas entered her mind.

158

Ebbing and flowing energy, he scanned her mental field. It felt empty, like a hollow cavity.

Hey, listen, Thomas traced. *You have to know by now that I come and go as I please. What's the point of pretending with me? You ever think what we could do if we were to join forces? Ticey?*

He studied her mind—all of her thought and will, feeling, judgment—all that was conscious.

Justice? he traced more formally, thinking that she might not have liked the nickname.

She seemed not to hear him or to know he was there. If it were possible for him as force and energy to smile grimly, he did so now.

All right, he traced. *Now I'm talking to* you, *whatever you are. I know it was you watching! Justice's watch-guard, that's who you are. What kind of thing are you if you have to control her so hard? Why don't you let her free to choose her own partner?*

THE WAY YOU ALLOW LEVI FREEDOM TO CHOOSE?

These words stood out in his own senses quite large. He had no reason to believe he hadn't thought them himself. They were like something he might tell himself in all honesty. Yet he had a strong suspicion that the words had been planted.

Thomas probed Justice's nerve substance. He scanned regions of contact between nerve cells and the impulses which passed across them. He found that her mind was not sick or damaged in any way that he could tell. But the sensation that expanded throughout her nervous system was what he called empty or hollow.

So, okay, he traced.

With his telepathic network totally in touch with her

159

senses, he soon knew how she struggled to get the snake inside her knapsack. An awful, foul odor came from the snake. And swiftly Thomas broke contact with Justice.

Someone should tell her that that big a snake will stink up the joint for twenty-four hours. Garters can give off a smell like that when they feel threatened. This he projected to whatever it was might be watching. He thought this for whatever might be listening in on him.

There was no response.

Okay, he traced, to no one in particular. *But I know you're somewhere. And, for all I know, you are Ticey with a lot more going than I ever thought. But why doesn't she know what the snake race is? Huh? Tell me that. If she had extra-sensory, she'd-a known. So. You have to be some kind of control watching after all. Because she* does *have extra-senory, she* has *to. And if you don't show yourself, I'm gonna embarrass her right in front of the boys!* He leaped inside Ticey's brain to scan.

There was no surge, no radiant energy to show that anything had heard him.

You gonna let her get all embarrassed and feel like a worm, Thomas traced. *You gonna keep her an ordinary kid for a while—why?*

There was no response that he could sense. But he was hot and sweating, standing once again on the ground. He was watching his sister close her knapsack over this oversized garter and he was back in his own head. The contact with Justice had been broken.

You threw me out! Who are you to throw me out?

He was stunned by the smoothness with which something, the watch-guard, the control, had thrown him out of Justice's mind.

Oh, so you threw me out because I was a threat!

YOU WERE THROWN OUT TO SHOW YOU ARE NO THREAT.

What thought that? Thomas wondered. That something might be able to implant words in his own brain made him cringe with fear.

Nah, I just thought it myself.

Apprehensively, he glanced all around the shade, at the river water, sluggish and thick with bracken. *Taking advantage, throwing me out when I'm busy thinking things over.* He sent this message across to Ticey's mind in the hope it would get through to the control. But he didn't quite believe that Ticey had anything inside her more than the power he had. So, in order to ease him out, it must have been Ticey herself who had caught him unawares.

I haven't yet been tested. In case there was a control: *I haven't tried my hand full force, not yet I haven't. Keeping it a secret from Mom and Dad. Not to give them a clue. Mom suspects, but she'll try not to believe what she knows. She and Dad are mostly okay. I don't have it in for either one of 'em. But that stupid, dumb Levi! Man, what a mess!* Thomas traced. *And weak-kneed. Why he has to look like me, man? And following me around—he followed me into this world! That's why I make up monsters and black and screaming places so he'll have to live in them. Yeow!*

Inwardly, Thomas laughed. *And keep him away from Ticey while she caught the snake; so I could watch her without him butting in.* Abruptly, he let his telepathy fade.

Justice had finished her job. It had given her the shivers. She felt clammy all over, but she had done it—the biggest snake anybody could find! She turned away from the Trace and discovered Thomas.

"It was you I saw come up here—you been here all this time?" she asked him.

He felt that the obvious needed no answer. "C-c-come *on,*" he stammered.

His voice sounded brutal. She was aware that the two of them were completely cut off from the others. Levi. Justice hurried by Thomas with her eyes averted. She was so afraid he would start in about how she had been a fool to try a trick on the dangerous Quinella Road. But he kept his mouth shut, she was glad of that. Around the bend and through clumps of snakes, amidst heat and dust, Thomas never said a word. Up ahead of them, closer to her than the other boys, Justice spied Levi peering out, as though he would see around the bend.

"You all right?" he said, so relieved to see her.

"Sure!" she answered, smiling brightly at him.

You two shouldn't be allowed on the same planet, Thomas traced to Levi. *I swear, when you and Tice get together, you're sickening.*

You just leave her alone or I'll . . .

You'll what? Thomas traced. *I'm gonna do anything to her. She's gonna do it to herself.*

Levi clamped his mouth shut even more tightly, determined not to argue with his brother. Justice thought his eyes seemed afraid for a split second.

"Levi? I got this snake."

He had turned and was walking back toward the other boys. Justice caught up and skipped at his side. She held up her knapsack. Levi stopped in his tracks. The other boys were coming toward them.

Thomas got between the boys and Levi. His back was to the boys as they came up. He faced Justice and Levi. She was still holding up her knapsack for Levi to see. He was staring at it with his lips slightly parted.

162

"What took you so long?" one of the boys said to Thomas, and then looked shocked at his own bravery. They all had bunched around him, gingerly holding peanut-butter pails full of creatures writhing darkly.

"Get these snakes to the field," someone else said. "Boy, I hope we don't have to do this ever again."

"Yeah," Talley Williams said, "I bet you get warts from handling snakes, just like you get them from frogs."

"Toads," Dorian said softly.

"Sh-sh-shut up, youuu g-guys!" Thomas yelled.

Suddenly, Levi pulled himself up in rigid attention. He began speaking rapidly:

"Frogs—or—toads—don't—cause—warts." With words spaced evenly: "Warts—are—caused—by—a—virus. A—virus."

Thomas grinned an ugly smirk. The boys stared at Levi. Justice wondered why he was sounding like a robot, or had she imagined it? Was he being funny? But Levi hardly ever was funny in that way.

All at once, Levi's shoulders slumped and he hung his head.

"Wh-whaaat's in-in the *bag?*" Thomas said to Justice. He swiveled around, turning the boys' attention away from Levi to her.

"Huh?" she said. "Oh," glancing at the sack, holding it higher for them to see.

The boys shuffled closer. "Is that what I think it is?" Talley Williams said.

"Bet it's the biggest snake *you* ever saw," she told him. "See?" She jiggled the knapsack and the form slithered in a whipping motion.

She felt as though she'd won a prize. Now she'd made

up for wrecking over there on the road. Boys all standing around watching the biggest creature anybody'd ever seen.

"See?" she repeated triumphantly.

"Just only one snake?" asked a boy named Bobby Matthews. Justice had never cared for him.

The boys turned to one another. There were strange looks, as though something odd had dawned on them. *"One* snake?" someone else said.

Tittering back in the group. A loud guffaw.

She lowered the knapsack. It held an odor, but she was hardly aware of it. She glanced at Levi, who had his head down, turned away from all of them.

"The bigger the snake," she said softly, "well, the faster it'll go when I race it in The Great Snake Race."

There was a moment of silence in which each boy seemed to be holding his breath. The next instant, all of the boys burst out laughing, jostling one another and grinning, lightly punching Thomas' arm. Thomas shrugged and grinned back at them.

"Is she crazy? Man, girl, you are crazy!"

Like slaps in the face. Wounding her.

Thomas leaned out of the group toward Levi: "Tuh-tuh-told you she'd *do* it a-a-ll hhherself."

"What are you laughing at?" she whispered. "What is wrong with you all?"

Her throat had become thick and full. Seeing her cringing before them, boys realized she didn't yet know what was going on.

"It's not racing snakes," Slick told her, laughter still in his voice.

And, kindly, Dorian said, "Tice, it's to see who can capture the most. It's the highest number of them any one

164

person can get. That's what makes the winner. We don't race them against each other."

Stillness, in which Thomas turned on his heel and walked away. The boys, feeling uncomfortable, turned away also.

Justice's face turned pale and she felt she would melt away. She was numb all over; she was dumb. Defeated. But she wouldn't cry, not now, not any time.

They can't make me.

Levi raised his head, watching Thomas and the boys trudge away. He looked wretched, worse than Justice felt. His face contorted in fury. His chest heaved up and down.

"I hate him," he said. "I hate him. I hate him."

After that, he got hold of himself and started back toward the field, with Justice beside him.

"Why didn't somebody tell me it wasn't racing the snakes?" she asked.

"Who would've thought someone would think it was?" Levi said. He laughed bitterly. "You can't blame him for taking advantage of your ignorance. Thomas'll take advantage of anyone, but you in particular. Oh, I don't know. I don't know where it's all going to end!

"We're freaks, you know," he added, quite clearly, so there was no mistaking what he said. "Thomas and me are."

"You are not, now stop it!" Justice said. She was shocked. "It's that Thomas doesn't like me very much at all."

Levi turned to her. He studied her for a moment, stopping still, searching her face. "I always hoped, because of your name," he began. "I don't think your name was an accident—" He left off, shook his head and sighed. "We're freaks. Maybe you are, too."

They went on. Justice thought she heard him say under his breath: "I won't live long, either. I'm glad."

165

Somewhere within her, suddenly, was the Watcher, who calmed her without her knowing. Had her tell herself without her knowing: "Brother of mine, you'll live. I'll see to that."

Undisturbed, Justice walked on with her favorite identical next to her, and carrying her snake larger than all the rest.

10

All day, boys went quietly within the hedgerow, checking on containers of wiggling, twining creatures. Times the creatures would be still, feeling cool, perhaps, and growing accustomed in the row's shaded stillness. Then, suddenly, they would seem to heave up in unison, as if knowing through shared sensations that this ancient place was not their home.

Justice made trips to her snake throughout the day. She kept the knapsack damp by filling a cup with tap water and carrying it out to the row. She'd let the water sit until it was the same temperature as the surrounding air. Then she'd wet the outside of the knapsack, carefully, so as not to disturb her snake.

Hope that's right, she thought. No one says what's right anymore, not even Levi. She felt disappointment rise and fade and rise again as the day turned.

Never one to quit, she would have to ask questions. What do you think the word *race* means? she had asked at the day's end.

"Why, the color of a people," her mom had said.

"No, not that kind of a race. I mean a foot race." Justice had made it easy for her mom to naturally say a race is a certain kind of contest.

"Well, then, it's a contest . . ."

Yes!

". . . to see which one will win," her mom said.

"Sure it is!" Justice was quick to agree. "And if you were to race raccoons, say?"

"What? Who would know how to race raccoons?" her mom asked.

"Mom . . ."

"Oh, I see, it's hypothetical."

Whatever that means.

"Well, then," her mom said, "it would be a contest to see which raccoon came in first."

That's what *I* thought, Justice had told her mom.

"But then," her mom had said, "how are you going to tell raccoons apart? You'd have to tag them, and if I know anything about wild raccoons— Maybe it's to see how many of them a person can—"

"No!" Justice cut in on her, so angry at her mom she couldn't get another word out. And she sashayed from the room.

I'll get Dad, she'd thought to herself. When she'd got him, he said just about what she had wanted him to say.

"Race?" he'd questioned. "You mean like 'I'll race you to the corner,' like in a contest?"

"Yeah, like that," Justice told him.

She loved the way her dad talked things, slow and easy. There were pauses between his words, as though each was a heavy stone and he had picked it up to see it, to know its shape and weight before he used it.

Being so close to her dad gave her a sudden fear she might lose him. She had to hold herself tightly inside and tell herself how foolish she was being to keep from crying.

Don't know what's gotten into me, she thought. But she knew; knew why she had to go around asking her friends the meaning of *race*. Her friends she could count on one hand. Her mom and dad and Mrs. Jefferson.

And went down there to see Mrs. Jefferson long before her mom and and dad came home and she asked them about *race*; and after she had checked on her snake for the twentieth time to make sure it was safe and sound. It lay so still, but she could tell it was alive. She'd gone down to Mrs. Jefferson's when there had been no boys in the hedgerow as she walked through. She saw all the peanut-butter buckets hung from tree limbs like lanterns along an old-fashioned avenue. She felt like taking the tops off and letting the snakes loose.

You don't win a race by cheating.

I'm going to win. It wasn't possible she could win, she knew that. Not unless she could get grown-ups to say a race had to be a contest of one against another, racing. She didn't know how she could ever do that without telling on both her brothers, how they had these snakes in the hedgerow. If she did that, she'd be out of favor forever. But wasn't it forever now?

And in that Jefferson place of magical green like no other, Justice found she could ask her question in a voice of soft willow: What must a race mean?

Dorian, having to look away from her and the wind that swooshed around her.

"Don't let the child worry," was Mrs. Jefferson saying from somewhere. Justice couldn't see her; yet she recognized the voice as that of the Sensitive.

Who are you talking to? was what Justice thought.

"He who allows tricks to be played will be punished," said the Sensitive.

Who? Justice wanted to know.

169

"But how was I to figure she didn't understand what a snake race was?" said Dorian.

"Not you," said the Sensitive. "Although you could have probed her thought."

"I couldn't," he said. "Because I didn't doubt she knew. And anyway Tom-Tom had a trace in on her. He would've found me out."

"He will be punished for playing tricks," said the Sensitive.

"I won't have Thomas hurt," Justice said. Even as she spoke, she was aware of Thomas hurting and Levi hurting. Somewhere, the future and the river. Water and hurting. Times to come and Thomas' ending.

"I don't want to see," she said.

"You can't help seeing," said the Sensitive. "Your way is clear with far sight."

"Is that what it is in me watchful and out there, wind green?" Justice asked.

"It's not nothing terrible," whispered the Sensitive. "It's a great given. It's a given greater than any I've seen."

Justice turned her face to the Sensitive. All this time, her eyes had been rolled back in their sockets and only the whites showed.

"You've told me something," Justice said, "something important."

"Have I? I may have," said the Sensitive.

"I will remember. No greater given."

"This is true, as far as I've seen," said the Sensitive. She got up from her chair and, quite heavily, knelt on the floor before Justice. Dorian stood at his mother's side. He looked at her and then at Justice, with great tenderness. Gently, Justice stroked his mother's cheek with her fingers.

170

They were silent a long time. At last, Justice said, "I will care for Dorian," and that was all.

"Thank you," said the Sensitive. She rose, taking her place again at the table. "In this life, I am your servant to give you what help I can."

Justice's brown eyes came into focus on her hands lightly touching the hand of Mrs. Jefferson on one side of her and that of Dorian on the other. She slid her hands from theirs and stood up. The room was faintly green for her. She made up her mind to leave.

"Have I had your fruit salad yet?" Justice asked.

"I didn't make it today," Mrs. Jefferson said. "I can't make it every day, child."

Mrs. Jefferson didn't smile. She had entered Justice's mind already to put in place the veil of forgetfulness. She couldn't help wondering when would come the day that Justice would leave this house knowing of her own power.

Justice left mumbling her goodbyes. She did not yet know her power; but she knew something.

Nearing the end of that day in her room. Without words or thoughts, she knew she was no longer herself. Somewhere within, she gathered and grew beyond who she had been. She understood that she was growing up. And then she gathered more, as a snail's pace.

Finding out, not in words or thoughts, but through an awful sense within her of being abandoned, that she would never be the same after this day.

Rather than cry out, cut off from her family in her room, she slipped down the hall to find her mom. Not knowing where the boys were, she perceived they weren't in the house. There wasn't a live trace of them—no echo of breathing or heartbeats. There were signals of the boys having been in the house less than a half-hour ago. Red and yellow touches of the boys on walls and furniture; prints of their fingers trailing along windowsills. They were like scents, these color signals.

She found her mom rushing about the house, putting it in order.

"I have so little time for this," she told Justice, sounding relieved.

Justice joined the rush, slipping her arm through her mom's as they went from one room to straighten another. Being close to her mom was sadness. Was knowing through a thickness in her throat that this would be the last time they would be this sort of alone together.

What's happening to me? thought Justice. It was Levi said he wouldn't live long. But is it me, too, dying?

Not in words but in flashes of swelling intelligence came to her her first impression of the Watcher. *No, you are not dying.*

She and her mom sorted laundry in what was called the mud room. It had been a pantry and was now converted into a service area with an exit door to the outside. All through the wet months of winter and spring, the family entered and left the house by this mud-room door. It was one of many sensible habits that made the house a home. Doing the same thing day after day caused a safe feeling to grow inside Justice.

"You mind doing this all the time?" abruptly she asked her mom. She eyed the piles of dirty laundry her mom sorted into whites and colors. Justice began helping.

"Yes, I guess I do mind some," her mom said. "I mean, I get angry when I come home from a hard day and you

172

all are sitting around, and all the laundry is here waiting for my common touch."

"But you never once asked us to do it or showed us how," Justice said.

"I know." Her mom's hands were busy flipping clothes into the washer. "I haven't been an 'away' mom long enough to divide up the chores," she said. "I guess I thought you guys would ask to do the work that had to be done. I was a dope."

"I'm glad to help," Justice told her. "Bet Levi would be, too." She gazed at her mom. "I'd be just glad to help forever."

Surprised and touched, her mom dropped what she was doing to clasp Justice's curly head to her chest. And planted a smacking kiss on her forehead.

"You sound so grown-up sometimes," her mom told her.

They stood there, folded peaceably against one another, until Justice had to ask her question about *race* and got the wrong answer. She sashayed away. And best she did, too, before her mom could wonder why she was such a clinging vine today.

Because boys are so cruel, that's why I want to be with her, Justice thought. Thomas. Because I have not one girl-friend. And never will, either. Not now.

She knew this. Not from the sound of words, but from deep sorrow of losing—races. Time. Herself.

When her dad came home near the supper hour, she was distressed and bewildered at herself. She paced the house, biting her hands and sucking her fingers. The boys were back and in their room. One of them came through, going past her. She couldn't tell which one of them it was. He, whichever he was, stared at her while passing, but never said anything to her. She knew she must look a sight, so upset, eating her hands. Her hair was a mess, looking as is she'd slept badly on it, when actually she hadn't had a nap all day.

But then her dad came home. She went out to the battered Oldsmobile, not only to meet him, but to get to him first before anyone else could take his attention from her.

Heat poured out of her in odorous sweat. She pulled at the door handle on the driver's side. Her dad, sitting there, was turning off things. He stared up at her.

"Ticey," he said, as the motor died. Eyelids dried out, his eyes were red and strained.

Frantically, she pulled at the door handle.

"Take it easy!" her dad said. He pulled up the door lock. It was then she recalled the door would not stay closed unless locked. Now it gave a squeaking sigh and swung open. Her dad lifted one leg out of the car. She grabbed his arm and began pulling him. She left off when she couldn't move faster than he wished to go.

The back seat of the car had space full of her dad's tools. All sorts of heavy things for scraping, sizing, breaking. Mallets, rulers, levels and planes. A massive iron sledgehammer. They never went riding in the car these days. Silver-gray ladders were tied to the car's roof.

Her dad out of the car and she was hanging on his arm.

"You will get the cement dust all over you," he said firmly to her.

It was then she saw that her dad was covered from head to foot with a fine whitish powder.

"But you're a stone man," she thought to say.

"I know it," he said, "and what's to hold the stones together?"

174

"Oh. Cement, I guess," she said.

She held tightly to her dad even when he turned toward the steps. She tried pulling him back, but he shook her off with some amount of force. She was hurt by what she thought was his wanting to be rid of her.

"Dad?" an anguished cry.

"Ticey," he said, with a tremor there under the word, "I am beat to my socks and I need a shower before dinner."

He turned from her to climb the steps. Stiffness in his legs. His back obviously hurting. She imagined she saw his hands tremble.

"Dad? Are you getting old?" And such pain and sorrow in her voice, her dad never really heard the words.

"What? Ticey, what is it?"

He turned back to her, standing there just above the steps in something close to a crouch, as if he would drop from tiredness. He had heard the cry of a child, lost, and he dropped down to the top step to sit, breathing deeply. Justice was there beside him in an instant. She took hold of his arm and commenced rubbing her face along the sleeve of his dusty workshirt. When she looked up at him again, she wore a mustache of fine powder.

Her dad grinned at the sight. "Ticey, girl," he said. And then: "The boys been at you again?"

"The identicals," she said.

"Oh, so that's how it is," he said.

And she spoke softly back: "You just remember—" Making up her mind to hold in the sadness she felt: "—remember, I was your only daughter."

Sitting still, carved dark and damp from heat, her dad stared down at her.

She could feel his whole self alert to her now as he cupped her chin in his hand. Her mouth quivering, and she took a moment to make it stop.

"What's this all about?" he said.

By no means to tell him or ever show him. What he was able to see was his only daughter looking peaked and upset. Her veiled, dark eyes bore into him; and all of his father's know-how and be-all could not penetrate them.

"You've always been my only daughter, Ticey. And you always will be, you know that. Come on, now."

"You leave me so alone," she said in a whimpering, like a child.

He understood her to mean her mother as well. "No, we don't," he said. "I work. And your mother goes to school. It's us doing what we have to do."

"I don't fit into it. I won't get another chance," she whispered.

"Ticey, I don't like the sound of that," he said. "Cut it out, now. No need to do anything silly." Staring at her, he studied her to see if he could figure what was behind all of this talk of hers. It was so easy to take a child lightly. He weighed possibilities in silence. Tired to his bones, he gambled on Justice's good sense.

"We're not going to solve a single world problem sitting here," he said, joking, and got unsteadily to his feet. "Come on with me," he told her.

But Justice took his hand and pulled him down to sit a minute more. It was then she asked him about *race* and got the answer she wanted, just to comfort herself.

"Come on in with me and your mom," he said. But she chose to stay where she was. She waved him bye-bye. He smiled and went on in. She did not see him frown as he turned away.

176

Inside, with heat rolling off him, with no relief from it anywhere in the house. The fans droned. He found his wife in the kitchen, greeted her with a silent kiss between them.

"I'm in the shower already," he told her, turning on his heel.

"Well, you needn't rush off."

"If I don't, I might gobble the supper before supper, and the cook, too."

"You had a pleasant day, I see," she said.

"Nice amount of work, though hard in the heat," he told her. "It'll last half the winter, too."

"Oh, well, then, I get a new coat and Ticey does, too," she told him.

"That's what I meant to tell you," he said. "I'm so beat, I forgot it walking from the front door to here."

"Forgot what?"

"Ticey," he said.

"What about her?" Mrs. Douglass asked.

"Keep an eye on her is all. Or have Levi to. She's thinking about running away."

"What? But that's not possible," Mrs. Douglass said. "Just a while ago, she was saying she wanted to help me . . . to be with me forever."

"Well." Mr. Douglass cleared his throat. "Something's got her spooked. I don't mean to press you . . ."

"Don't, then," she said.

"But maybe Ticey's too young to be left here with the boys all day."

"You want me to give up school?" Mrs. Douglass asked.

"I never said that."

"But that's what you meant."

Mr. Douglass sighed. "Just only that maybe we can get

some help for us around here. Someone young in the house with Ticey."

"You mean paid help?" Mrs. Douglass said.

"Know another kind?"

"We can't afford to pay someone to do what I do in this house," she said. And began to slowly burn; pots and pans suddenly were loud in her hands.

"Well," he said again. A pause. He started through the door. "Will take that shower now." And left her standing there with her anger and her guilt.

No sooner did she feel guilty about leaving Ticey alone all day than she felt frightened. She began to wonder if maybe Ticey was planning something foolish.

I don't know what it is, she thought. But she knew something was wrong somewhere in the family. She tended to blame herself when anything upset the home system. She had an inkling of something troubling deep in her mind. Yet she had no real time to think, to put her finger on what it was; else, she didn't want to.

"What's wrong with me?" she wondered out loud. Maybe something's wrong with this marriage, she thought, and dismissed it at once.

Working again, cooking now, she saw that her preparations were as thorough and as smooth as ever. She worked steadily, pulling the meal quickly together, spending as little time as possible. Still, it would be a good meal —swiss steak, rice seasoned in beef bouillon. Salad.

"Why blame me?" she whispered.

Nevertheless, throughout the rest of the evening, she was quick to take offense at anything her husband jokingly said. And she kept Justice close to home.

Night came and they went to bed. The house was still,

utterly. Mrs. Douglass woke several times and tiptoed to Justice's room. Every time, she found her child deeply asleep.

A long interval of dreams and silence surrounding them, after which Mrs. Douglass awoke with a start, her mind at once alert. She lay on hot, damp bedding in her own perspiration.

And all the windows open, she thought. God, when will this weather break?

It isn't weather, she thought. Weather changes.

She would not let her imagination leap to the incredible thought of rainless years. She lay still, hoping for some breath of a breeze. None came. Glancing at her husband beside her, she found him log-like and deep asleep. Then she lay still, breathing as softly as she could in order to hear the house. She knew it had a life of its own. All good houses did. She could say this to herself, although she wouldn't say it to anyone else. There were houses that held on to their history of love and laughter. Banged fingers, stomachaches cured with rocking; babies squealing with delight. Grown-up arguments; that faithful formality grown serene between adults who have cared for one another over many years. All of it seeped beneath the floorboards and behind the walls.

Now the house breathed its own life of calm and quiet. The best time to hear it, to know it, was this time, deep in the night. She listened, alert to human sound, and to the creaking of old wood which never quite died away.

She heard Levi snoring softly. Sinuses, she thought. I'll have to have them looked after.

Thomas made no steady sounds, although he occasionally laughed or yelled out, dreaming. She listened, but heard nothing from him. Yet, strangely, she imagined she saw him moving about. Silliness, she told herself.

Mr. Douglass' warning about Justice running away broke the peace.

Why didn't I wake up sooner? How could I have forgotten!

She was out of bed in an instant and making her way to the hall. Justice's room was the first on the opposite side from the parents' bedroom. The boys' room was a few paces farther away, on the other side of Justice's room, closer to the parlor.

What greeted her there in the hall paralyzed her judgment. What she felt was a power of watching coming from Justice's room into the hall. An enormously tranquil observing, which appeared to blink, as would human eyes.

The Watcher steadied now on something against the wall. It was Thomas, caught in the light of awareness— Mrs. Douglass imagined she could see him through the dark. The Watcher fixed on his terror-stricken expression and drew him away down the hall. He floated through the darkness and through the doorway of his room.

Mrs. Douglass felt quite peaceful. She wondered momentarily why she stood in the hall. She had the impression she had checked on Justice and had found her daughter all right. Now she turned and went back to bed.

She lay with her cheek on the pillow, feeling a mantle of fresh air pass over her shoulders. It cooled the bedding, cooled her bare legs and arms.

The Watcher brought the coolness and left it a long time in the parents' room. Until Mrs. Douglass slept soundly, with no feeling of time or dreams.

11

The sun had not risen; yet there was a thick, milky paling of the fading night. Air was heavy with the scent of honeysuckle, which grew in high mounds near the house. The cottonwood tree was full of darkness. Its leaves were blackened, still, and withered from the heat and the prolonged dry spell. Justice could hardly realize that she had a special feeling for it only a couple of days ago.

"Cottonwoman" sounded faintly somewhere inside her, but her delight was all but gone.

They had come outside as soon as the east showed the change of dawning. But first they had dressed soundlessly in their rooms. Thomas and Levi had communicated in their minds so as not to chance waking their folks.

You think Justice got herself up on time? Levi had traced to Thomas.

She's up and out by the front already, Thomas traced back.

You heard her when she went out? Levi had looked alarmed. If Thomas had heard Justice leave, his folks might have, also. A tremor of revulsion passed over him. Even though they had been mind-tracing, he'd forgotten about himself and his brother. For there were times, such as this morning, when he awakened thinking they were ordinary boys. Then he would shudder suddenly, as he had just now, when he remembered he and his brother had their loathsome talent. Thomas could intercept movement, even thought fragments through walls and closed doors. That's how he knew Justice was outdoors. And Levi was doomed forever to be a partner in his brother's telepathic crimes.

Thomas was in one of his moods. Not just foul, but deadly cold. He had awakened, he told Levi, to find himself stiff and aching, half under his bed.

Did you have something to do with it? Thomas traced to his brother as they left the house.

I was sleeping, you know I was.

How can I know that when I was asleep, too? Thomas traced. His mouth was a grim line as he silently opened the front door. Sometime during the night—he figured it was about three or so—he'd got out of bed to take a look at Ticey while she was dead asleep. Maybe to give her a few dreams, the kind he sometimes suggested to the sleeping Levi. And maybe to see if there was anything he could find out about her while her mind was in an unconscious state. Thomas thought he remembered getting out of bed and going down the hall. But after that, everything was a blank. Maybe he'd slept, had nightmares—he didn't know, and not knowing made him suspicious. He had found himself in the morning on the floor. He had been twisted and cramped, as if he'd been flung there, half under the bed.

The three of them now stood on the drive in the thick, murky light before dawn. Their dad's battered Olds and their mom's rusty red Vega were lumps of the same gray. Justice thought to look behind them far to the west where there was darkness still. She'd never been up so early and she was delighted to see how the night was banished by sunrise.

182

"When will the sun come up?" she whispered to Levi.

"Shhh!" Thomas warned, so furious at her talking he nearly hit her. They had to get away from the house; he walked a few paces away, with them following.

"Take the bikes through the side yard and down the garden to the gate," Thomas told them. He spoke right in their faces, so close they could feel his morning breath. "Take them down the field and lay 'em toward Dorian's until we need them."

"When will we need them?" Justice asked him, without thinking.

In the pale dawning, Thomas' anger was like a contorted atmosphere covering his features. Justice slapped her hand over her mouth and stared at the ground.

Hastily, Levi led her over to her bike and lifted the stand with his hand for her, rather than kicking it up. "Start on out," he whispered. "Be quiet as you can!"

She started out, with Levi following her, his own bike in hand, and with Thomas bringing up the rear.

They moved cautiously. Within the fence separating them from the field, the garden was still a night garden. Roses, cornflowers and orange California poppies were drab and colorless. Tomatoes hung like ebony balls from gray plants. Melons were clumps of dead shapes on the ground.

At the closed gate, Justice grew aware of something gathered on the other side. She heard no sound. But she sensed shadow. It was more of a substance than the darkened garden. It raced for the hedgerow.

Levi reached around her to open the gate expertly, with little sound. They went through with their bikes and on down the field into rising soft light scented with clover. The light gave grass its green as they walked through it, while, all around, blackened houses, weeds and bushes were still night-full.

They laid their bikes neatly at the far end of the field, Justice's on the side next to Levi's. She stared at the two sleek black bikes and her own less streamlined, slower one. Everything, even the air, held an importance that she could not quite comprehend. She sensed four-leaf clovers everywhere, sensed through them and lost the sense of what they were. Moments came and passed when she knew beyond, and no longer knew, what was the sweet odor that filled her nostrils.

They turned back and headed up the field. Dawn had risen to the height and quality of shade. The sky to the east was streaked orange with luminous ribbons of cloud. As the streaks grew brighter, the ribbons dissolved before their eyes. Justice saw leaves of the cottonwood catch the light and turn silver. To the west, light rising drove the night far beyond the line of the ancient trees.

There among the hedgerow's thousands of leaves she saw heads, a shirtfront, trouser legs. Faces, wary and pale, peeked and watched them make their way toward the row by the fence. They made her gasp in shocked surprise; it was like a scream in the stillness.

Thomas shoved her violently forward, furious at her noise, nearly knocking her down. Her arms flailed wildly until she regained her balance.

"If you don't quit!" Hardly a sound he made on the air.

Justice took a deep breath and held herself in. Levi had her firmly by the arm now. But she shook him off and scrunched her shoulders high so she wouldn't do anything else wrong.

At the edge of the row, they slipped through the young,

184

volunteer trees. There was dampness covering these morning trees. Yet Justice sensed that, over all, the hedgerow was quite dry. It came to her that, high up, leaves were turning brown and yellow, with fall still many weeks away.

I've lost, she thought, as she followed within the row. Hard, horizontal branches were arms of night reaching.

Her face flushed and she lowered her head to hide the shame, from trees, from boys, of having just one snake.

Quickly, now, The Great Snake Race began.

Up and down the row, under the stately arch of trees, boys stood at the ready by their lantern pails of snakes. Every boy held on to the branch above his pail. Each stood still and at full attention. Justice, seeing Levi take his place, took her place near him, with her knapsack hanging from its branch to the right of her head. She could not hold on to a branch as the others did without leaping up and hanging there by one arm. So she stood still where she was, arms to her sides.

Thomas hung there before them; had swung himself up onto a horizontal branch that rocked up and down from his weight. To Justice, he was a picture of Levi that someone had deliberately bent and creased and then taken a crayon to.

She noticed Dorian way down the row, looking small and far away. And had a vision in which he and the others were petrified figures of stone with dust filtering down on them from the vaulted height of the row.

She blinked rapidly. Saw dawn filter through the osage line and there was hardly any dust here within the heavy trees.

Thomas raised his arm straight up. Boys stood rigidly, without moving a muscle. Levi's attention was riveted on his identical. And for Justice, Thomas was the negative to the certain, clear image of her favorite brother. Thomas was light reversed. Shade, never to develop.

Thomas let his arm swoop down. At once, boys lifted down their containers from the branches.

Justice did the same.

Boys faded out from the row with Justice following.

Outside, it was sun-up with no coolness about it. Even the rising twitter and melody of birds seemed to sizzle. There was the rushing momentum of a few cars far down on Dayton Street.

Early Saturday, with most folks sleeping late. They would stir about nine. Fathers, robed and slippered, would then head for dens to wait for breakfast. On Saturday morning, few women slept late to be waited on. Mrs. Douglass was one of the few. She need not awaken before ten; her breakfast would be ready around ten-thirty. Sausage and silver-dollar wheatcakes. Juice and coffee. It had been so for as long as Justice could remember. She and her brothers would eat when they had a mind to, with Levi fixing, usually. This on any normal Saturday, which was every Saturday when there wasn't to be a Great Snake Race.

Now boys stayed close to the hedgerow for protection against the open field, bright with light. The Dayton Street houses looked back on the field; anyone awakened early would notice the boys and Justice crouching. Because of this, they were self-conscious, Justice particularly, and they scrunched low, backs to trees, to make themselves smaller.

Thomas motioned them into a circle there at the side of the field. It became a tight circle, with Justice squeezed in with Levi on one side of her and Dorian on the other

186

side. Boys didn't look at one another or at her. Their line curved away on both sides from Levi and Dorian to Thomas on the opposite side of the circle from Justice. Boys sat on their heels and so did Justice. They had their containers, and Justice, her knapsack, held close in their arms.

Thomas made a motion—a quick flip of his hand with index finger touching the ground.

Boys instantly set their containers in front of their knees. Justice set down the knapsack, holding firmly to the draw-strings. Boys settled back, stiff and straight; Justice had to lean forward somewhat, feeling a need to keep hold of her sack.

With head lowered, Thomas eyed the circle. "Slick," he said, in a sudden, soft hiss.

Slick Peru opened his peanut-butter container and turned it over. Boys leaned into the circle as snakes, stunned, began to writhe frantically in every direction.

"Sixteen," Slick said, "I counted 'em when I first put 'em in the bucket."

"Really?" Levi said, mildly surprised by the high number. Boys were snatching up snakes as the creatures crawled near them, and dropping them back into Slick's pail.

"Sixteen," agreed Talley Williams.

"Got it," said Levi. Justice didn't see him write it down. But she supposed when you got to be thirteen, you could remember most anything.

The Great Snake Race continued around the circle. Boys turned over their containers on the ground and called out their numbers of snakes after Thomas called their names: "Fourteen. Twelve. Ten. Fifteen—darn!"

After all of the boys' snakes had been collected again and put back in their separate containers, Slick Peru said softly, joyfully, "I win it! I win it! I mean, I think . . ." His voice trailed off as he became aware, realized—they all did, at about the same time—that Thomas had not called on Justice.

She had been trying to remember whether Dorian had ten or eleven snakes. She couldn't keep the numbers and boys straight to save her. And it dawned on her that the circle had grown quiet. Save for Thomas, all of the boys were staring at her.

The sun beat down, hot as blazes. Up there was a visible yellow-brown color of air-pollution sky. Was it fumes or earth dust from fields? Justice wondered. The top tier of the hedgerow was clearly discolored from dust or a serious lack of rain.

"Here, let me help you," Levi said to her, as though perhaps Thomas had told her something that she hadn't heard.

Levi loosened the drawstring of her knapsack. Justice felt the heat rise in her face and wished to be gone, anywhere but here. Having only a single snake was a pain, an awful pressure of embarrassment. She stole a look at Dorian. He played with his fingers, but he didn't seem to be made uncomfortable by her. He was ever keen and curious.

Justice had her face turned away from the circle. Without looking, she knew when Levi opened the knapsack and let her fine, large snake loose.

Oh, hadn't it been the perfect snake for a Great Snake Race!

Tears welled in her eyes. She swallowed and gritted her teeth, forcing them back.

So burning hot, I'll faint.

But she didn't faint. Cringing inside, she held herself stiffly in the circle.

The silence went on and on. Boys studying her ridiculous snake. She knew they had to be laughing, their hands over their mouths. And she was about to die, like a fool.

On and on, the silence.

Until there were murmurings, whisperings—"thirteen . . . fif . . . sixt . . ."

Boys slurring all kinds of numbers: "twenty-one, two, three . . ." A sudden tension and excitement in the air.

Justice swung her head around. Her jaw dropped; she sat stunned, her eyes huge, as boys still counted. "I don't believe it!" she squeaked.

"Thirty-nine, forty," Levi finished. "Who gets any more?"

"I get forty-one," Dorian said.

"I'm not finished, wait!" It was Talley, the most active counter after Levi.

Justice giggled, squealed softly. Eyes moist and bright, she hugged her arms around herself.

The grass in the circle flowed with crawling, perfect creatures. They were thin as rubber bands and only inches long. Down to their tiny serpent tongues, they were the exact stripe and coloring of the mother, the thick, large snake that Justice had so bravely captured.

"There's no rule I know of against having lots of babies," Levi said, about to burst with happiness. "Tice, I guess you win The Great Snake Race!"

"Whoopee!" she whispered, at last remembering to keep her voice down.

"Man!" boys whispered back.

"Shoot!" And laughter.

To her surprise, the boys didn't appear to mind that she had won. The whole thing had been such a comic shock.

"Man, a pregnant snake!" Slick said, and laughed again. "I thought they laid eggs."

"They do lay eggs," Levi said, "but inside their bodies, and they hatch inside, too."

"Man, I bet Ticey knew it all the time!"

She tried to look as though she had planned the birth of babies down to the best moment. She had learned from Thomas, and had promptly forgotten, that garter snakes birthed live babies.

Dorian grinned at her. Boys were looking at her admiringly. They good-naturedly handed over handfuls of tiny creatures. And Levi gingerly handled the sluggish mother snake to place it at the bottom of the knapsack.

"We need to get all of them back to the Trace soon," he said.

Justice was calming down. She listened to Levi and the other boys and had a sense of wonder at being accepted for the first time. She guessed a pack of boys was not much different from a bunch of girls. It was just harder getting their attention.

It hadn't occurred to her that they'd all have to take the snakes back.

Why not let them loose in the hedgerow? she wondered. No, because there's not enough water and it's not their home.

She had a vision of snakes let loose, slithering away down Dayton Street, clear across town and down the country road to the Quinella Trace. Cars screeching to a halt as the snakes slunk by. They would surely make one great snake race.

190

There was someone with her. Justice had a sudden notion that someone snide and unpleasant was sitting with her, inside her skin. She had no time to fear. No sooner had she noticed it than it commenced fading. She felt righteous anger at someone with her, uninvited. And sensed that it had intruded before. Having no experience, she reached out awkwardly with her will to catch it unawares.

Justice made contact. She grabbed hold of it inside and instantly felt its meanness and fury like searing heat. It fought her. They struggled; she sensed danger, but still she had no fear. She knew only that it was wrong for it to invade her mind. But finally she was forced to shield herself from its seething power. In furious triumph, it slipped away. Justice was left with a coolness inside.

Something is new.

Seeing the circle again—Levi and the boys. Only seconds had passed, if time had continued at all, in which Thomas across from her had made no impression on her. He had become a blank, as if he had gone away somewhere. Now Justice saw him again and gave him the faintest nod.

Something. She reached for him clumsily with her will. *I am knowing, Thomas.* Once more, she made contact with unpleasant heat.

Well, fer . . . Look who's here! You dumb, stupid girl, finally caught on, Thomas traced.

Thomas, it was you, wasn't it? she traced, but Thomas ignored her.

Lee? Didn't I tell you she had extra-sensory just like us? I knew she had it!

Once called, Levi was made aware of Justice within Thomas' mind. *Ticey!* he traced.

Levi! She willed herself over to Levi's brain. *Excuse me . . . entering without asking . . .*

It's okay, he traced.

I am . . . something. Awkwardly, Justice gathered power and skill to trace: *I am . . . new!*

Oh, fer— Will you listen to her drivel, fer Chrissakes! Thomas traced. *And no girl as dumb as her wins my Great Snake Race. Lee, you hear me? Slick wins it, I say so, and we give him a prize of something under five bucks. You better tell him, too, 'cause if you don't, I'll boil your brains!* His face grew dark in an explosion of rage.

Levi had a sickening, outrageous sensation that his brain rested in a pot over a fire as yet unlit.

Thomas turned his burning eyes on Justice. She felt unknown forces, new, gather inside her to protect her. Closing Thomas out, she projected a warning to Levi, urging him to say nothing to Slick Peru.

Give me some time, she traced to Levi. *I think . . . I am . . . not . . .* With an indescribable feeling of becoming new.

Levi was numb with fear. It had all happened too fast and he'd had no time, even, to be amazed at the surfacing of Justice's power. But the shock of discovering her in his mind was as disturbing as the illusion of his brain in a pot of water set to boil. If he told Slick, he might bring down Justice's wrath; for he had no way of knowing whether her power was a gift or, like Thomas', a punishment. And if he didn't do as Thomas had commanded, he knew exactly what Thomas would do to him.

Thomas added vegetables to the pot and seasoned the brain stew with fine herbs. Thomas lit a foot-long match.

Levi opened his mouth to tell Slick he had won.

No! Justice traced to Levi. Gracefully, she rose to her feet. Boys gave her their full attention, as though suddenly she had grown tall. They watched as she gathered up her knapsack full of snakes and cut straight across the circle past Thomas.

I win it, she traced to Thomas. *I'll lead the boys back to the Quinella.*

You think. You dumb . . . Not on your bloody life, you won't! he traced back.

They'll follow me. Justice made her way smoothly, easily, over to her bike.

Boys got to their feet, clutching snake pails, all eyes on Justice. In their eyes, she was still somehow less than a boy. But she had been smart enough to win The Great Snake Race fair and square. Wasn't that something! Justice and a pregnant snake! They figured she was on her way back to the Quinella. They'd tag along and empty out their own snakes. Why not?

Thomas knew better. Knew she had given the boys the same mental suggestion.

Stupid clowns, tracing to Levi and pulling Levi along as he traced to Justice. *Justice!* using her full name for the first time, he wasn't sure why. *You won't get away it with. Watch.*

She needn't turn to know what he was doing.

Boys headed for Justice stopped still. Looking all around, to the ground and up into the trees. What was the tremor they each felt? Why did they begin to shiver so in the sunlight?

"Did I hear thunder?" Talley Williams asked.

"Is it going to rain?" This from Bobby Matthews, with his grating voice. Justice had never cared for him.

Bobby Matthews felt stupid as sunlight continued to beat down in a cloudless sky. But he couldn't help shivering with cold, as did most of the other boys.

Levi was horrified by this expansion of Thomas' ability.

He'd never seen Thomas use such power, never known he had it and could use it on the boys. Unaware that Justice seemed to have the same ability, he must warn her to take care.

Justice! he thought, using her full name, but he had no ability to reach her.

He tried to get to his feet. But Thomas was right there in his mind, pretending to light the fire under the pot containing his brain.

Tom-Tom, don't! Levi traced.

You didn't tell Slick when I told you to, did you? Thomas reminded him.

But I was about to, desperately Levi traced back.

About to don't mean one thing. I'll remember that. Now, stay out of it.

Not all of the boys had responded to the illusion of tremor and fear that Thomas had telepathed to them.

So. Thomas slid from Levi's mind and pinned Dorian Jefferson like an insect in his sight. *It's you, the son of the spirit woman—you're one of us, too!*

In fear, shivering, Dorian stared back at Thomas. It was no use. He had been caught. Thomas could clearly sense that Dorian was not afraid.

He perceived something else. *You're different,* he traced. Thomas detected a veiled force protecting Dorian's mind from him. There must have been a similar shield protecting Justice for so long. Why, suddenly, had Justice's shield let down, revealing her not only to him but to herself as well?

That's maybe the way it works, Thomas thought to himself. Sometimes it works like that for me. I find out I can do something special when a minute before I didn't know a thing about it.

194

His attention was still riveted to Dorian, and he traced: *Know you're different. So how is it you're different from us? What can you do that's different? I'm just curious.* It was true. Thomas had long since ceased being in awe of his own power. He was not terribly surprised, in one day, to find two people who had similar power.

Dorian stood there. He looked over at Levi, who would not be able to get up until Thomas dissolved the illusion of his brain in a pot. He stared at Thomas, but could not penetrate his strong mental defenses.

Thomas had never observed Dorian in terms of extrasensory power. Now he looked at Dorian anew and wondered at his small, ragged appearance. Never in a million years would he have suspected.

Beautiful, Thomas traced. He smiled at Dorian. *I bet I find out everything pretty soon now. You watch and see, spirit boy! This is all-out war between me and Lee and you and that sister of mine!*

Abruptly, Dorian turned and headed away.

"Hey, you guys!" It was Justice, as ordinary as she could be. She was on her bike and calling from the side of the Jefferson house. It was a loud kind of whisper, like nothing Levi had heard before. He wasn't even sure he'd heard it, but he knew she'd called. The boys heard her. "You all afraid to go to the Quinella again? What's the matter with you!" She whirled and disappeared on her bike, successfully breaking Thomas' hold on the boys.

What were they doing standing there like a bunch of dumb bunnies? They couldn't imagine what had come over them, and they raced for their bikes parked in front of the Jefferson place—Dorian right with them.

At the side of the house, Dorian turned back to smile at

Thomas. It was his challenge, clearly in the cause of Justice.

The pot with the brain, the unlit fire, dissolved. Levi had his senses back. Unsteadily, he got to his feet.

Sorry, man, Thomas traced. It was easier for him to communicate telepathically and avoid his stutter. *I shouldn't have done that to you for so long. Didn't mean to. I just forget myself sometimes.*

Levi felt weak and light-headed. But he was deeply grateful for his brother's expression of sympathy. Thomas had never before apologized to him.

I can't take much more of it, Tom-Tom. It . . . it seems to upset my breathing, Levi traced.

Thomas was silent a moment. He knew already that his brother had a serious illness. Knew that it could only get worse. But he was powerless to do anything about it.

Well, I won't do it if you don't want, Thomas traced. *I mean, the crazy scenes I put in your mind. I only do it for fun, and I'm always right there with you.*

It's no fun for me, *I've told you that, Tom-Tom. You've got to start thinking about what you're doing.*

I know, and I will, too, I promise you. Come on, Thomas urged, *let's get the snakes back to the Quinella.*

No, I'd better get home, traced Levi. *I'm just so tired.*

Oh, come on! You'll feel a lot better with some wind in your face. Lee, the heat's got to you, is all.

Levi would have loved to sit under the trees and discuss Justice. But Thomas seemed in much too big a hurry for him even to suggest it.

If we race, we can catch them, Thomas traced eagerly. He led Levi over to his bike, making sure he got on all right. They headed out through the Jefferson driveway, with Levi bringing up the rear. As they passed Jefferson

196

windows, they both glanced up into the ever watchful gaze of Mrs. Leona Jefferson.

Veiled. Unreadable.

Levi nodded to her respectfully. Seeing her, he felt, strangely, less tired.

Thomas gave her a thumbs-up sign, smirking at her. She gave it back to him, thumbs down.

Stupid old spirit woman! So you hate my guts, so what? I don't need a spirit woman to weave spells over me, to shield me, or Levi, either. If Ticey's that weak, you'd best protect her because, man, when . . .

He broke off, remembering that Levi was in on the trace.

Once out in the street, he raced ahead before Levi could question him. Levi followed, pedaling evenly. It was true, biking on his racer down long, shaded streets into country soon revived him. He and Thomas caught up with Justice and the boys right after the B&O crossing. And they commenced a downhill race at spectacular speeds. Thomas moved up on Justice with Levi right behind him.

Justice didn't seem surprised to see Thomas. She gazed at him long and hard, then turned back to the road.

Levi intercepted no extra-sensory between them, which didn't mean they weren't locked in telepathic tracing. It could mean that Thomas hadn't seen fit to let Levi in on it.

Thomas grinned at Justice. He reached out, patting her arm, never diminishing speed. It was so like the way a guy would gesture good-naturedly to his buddy when they were having a swell time on a really pleasant day. But Thomas' open hand had knotted into a fist.

Levi couldn't believe his eyes as, in a flash, Thomas hit Justice a thudding blow on her arm. The impact sent her careening down the side of the road. The bike wobbled and took a long, frightening slide as Justice struggled to steady it and slow it down. It seemed to take her forever. Luckily, she hadn't fallen. As it was, the boys had a time slowing themselves and getting out of the way in case she lost control and came across the road.

Thomas had sped on away from them. By the time Justice had stopped the skid and had started her ride again, he was off his bike and racing for the Quinella Trace.

Boys were quiet now. They brought their bikes to a halt at the flat place in front of the fence.

"Did he hurt you?" Levi asked Justice.

She shook her head. *I* . . . She had opened telepathy between them and had begun to trace when she broke off.

She followed Levi over to the fence, next to which they laid their bikes. Boys stood around, still holding on to theirs, as if undecided whether to go or stay. They would not look directly at Levi or Justice. They felt they had intruded on some family argument, and Levi was quick to sense their predicament. There was no way for them to get around what they'd seen Thomas do. Thomas, their most exciting friend in the whole neighborhood. They were stunned by the danger, at him hitting Justice so hard, right in the midst of the bike traffic. But what got to them was that he had hit a younger, smaller *person* that hard; a girl who was also his sister. There was no excuse they could make for him, their glances at one another seemed to say. And they felt ashamed for him.

"We have to talk," softly Levi said to Justice. "We must talk!"

He wanted to trace to her, but he had no way to make his way into her thoughts without Thomas or her leading him through the strange, empty passage from mind to mind.

No need to talk, Justice traced. *Pardon me, but I am here.*

Tice . . . Justice!

Yes?

How's it possible that you kept all this from me?

I never knew! she traced. *And to think about it—to know that I have . . . have . . .* Even now, she could not bring herself to say it. Then: *Levi, why didn't you stay home? With you here, it makes it that much harder. . . .*

Makes what harder? What is it? he traced.

Don't you see? Thomas and I.

I understand about that, he traced, *but it doesn't have to be. Justice, Thomas loves to win, so let him. Don't fight him. I don't want to see you hurt.*

She smiled at him. No longer was it the smile of his little sister, but of someone older; beyond older. Someone different.

I am new, she said in his mind. *I am power. And awe . . .*

Awe? Levi traced. *What's that supposed to mean?*

This isn't the place—we'll have time later. Come, she traced. *Now, follow close to me. And never get between me and Thomas.*

I don't want to take sides, he traced.

She stared at him, looking troubled. She was aware of boys standing awkwardly, aware that they found the silence strained. And she decided the boys should leave.

They began whispering among themselves. None of them wanted to go back to the Quinella. It was agreed that Slick and Dorian would return all of the snakes. Slick balked at the idea of actually emptying the pails on the riverbank.

199

Instead, he said he would carry the snake pails only as far as the middle of the high weeds. So it was agreed that the center of the high weeds was good enough. The snakes would have no trouble finding their way back from there. Dorian would empty his containers in the weeds, as well.

Loaded with snake pails, Slick and Dorian climbed through the fence. Boys still held on to their bikes, ready for a fast getaway. And as soon as Slick was back, handing out empty containers, they prepared to leave. Testing hand brakes, sliding the pail handles through the handlebars. Then Slick and the boys raced up the hill and out of sight.

To leave Dorian like that? Levi wondered. They forgot all about him!

His next thought was that Justice had purposely made the boys forget and had also made them leave.

Yes, you're right both times, she traced, reading his thoughts.

"Thomas has that same kind of power of suggestion," Levi said out loud. He was more relaxed now that the boys were gone. "The first time I saw him use it was today on the boys."

"I know all about Thomas," she said. And in a voice at the edge of fear, "I'm learning all about me."

"Well, I wish there wouldn't be this battle between you," Levi said. "I'm glad I can't always be sighted the way you two are. Oh, Justice, why do we have this power—why us!"

"Let's not talk about it, if it upsets you. It upsets me, too," she told him. "Come."

She led the way. On the other side of the fence, Dorian waited for them in the high weeds. His alert, intelligent stare greeted Levi. Back in the field, Levi had understood through Thomas that Dorian had power. But none of them spoke of this now. He and Dorian stayed a pace behind Justice. The sun beat down on them and they felt snakes slither over their shoes, searching their way to the Quinella. Neither Justice nor Levi and Dorian looked up into the burning heat of sky. No need. There was hardly ever a cloud. For months, never any weather other than the relentless heat.

Three fourths of the way through the tall weeds, odors of rot and stagnant water rose around them. A moment later, Justice motioned to Levi and Dorian to stand still, as weird, unnatural images reached out for them.

12

Cautiously, Justice moved again. In the weeds on his left, Levi spotted an enormous rat the size of a panther. It fed on a mouthful of writhing, dying snakes and was headed directly for him.

Levi gasped and staggered in fear. Dorian, behind him, placed a hand gently on his shoulder. He felt as though his fear was draining away. And where there had been a huge, ferocious rodent, a mirage slowly faded.

It began to rain. It poured down in a fine coolness that grew stronger until it whipped at the high weeds, bending them nearly to the ground.

Levi laughed, shaking his wet hair, which was soon soaked through. "Oh, man!" he yelled. "Wow, rain at last!" He stuck out his tongue to drink some of it in. It was surprisingly bitter, and he clamped his mouth shut. His wet clothes seemed to tighten and cause an awful itching of his skin.

Again, Dorian's gentle hand pressed his shoulder. The sight and sound of rain vanished. The itching ceased and the bitter taste was gone. In disbelief, Levi watched his clothes dry in an instant, as though they'd never been wet. He looked to Justice, then Dorian. They had not had rain pour down on them, he realized.

Justice's eyes appeared lighter, flecked with blue, so cold were they with anger.

"Come," she said kindly, to Levi.

"Let me go home," he said weakly. He found himself sitting on the ground in the weeds. "How did I get down here? What happened?"

"These tricks of Tom-Tom's make you feverish," Dorian explained. "You fell right after the rain magic."

"I'll go home and lie down," Levi said.

"You're not strong enough to make it back up the hill," Justice told him. "You need rest. There under the shade trees is a good place for you to lie down for a half-hour. Then I'll deal with Thomas!"

"Don't hurt him, don't fight," Levi said. "He doesn't mean any harm, really. But he's never done it like this before, from outside my mind."

As Justice and Dorian helped Levi to his feet, Thomas' illusions came, one after the other.

Levi gasped for air as his windpipe opened and closed in spasms. Out of the sunlight came two large birds. Flapping yellow wings about his head, they picked at his eyebrows until they had plucked them clean. At the last, Levi ceased to exist. He couldn't see his arms stretched before him. When he tried to touch his own face, it, too, had disappeared. His fingers passed right through his chin and mouth.

"Where—?" Nothing was left. He was air, light, day. He was no longer.

"Justice, get me! Come find me! I'm gone, I'm out here somewhere. I can't find myself—help meee!"

He has power, traced Dorian to Justice, about Thomas. He and Justice still had Levi by the arms.

Yes, Thomas has power, Justice answered, but pushed back thoughts of her own strength growing. She was busy trying to get Levi to walk. *Pull him forward. You may have to lift his feet for him,* she traced. *We have to get him to the river and cool him with water.*

They could see through the air—Dorian and Justice—see where Thomas let loose his powerful images like silken sails. They had no choice but to let the images flow unhindered. To weave protection in Levi's mind while he was so weakened might cause him further damage. They had to get him to the shade where they could make him comfortable.

Thomas wants to hurt him, Dorian traced.

Maybe he only hopes to make me show myself, Justice traced back. *That's the reason he lured Levi back here. He must have—Levi was much too weakened to come on his own.*

You can't let it go on, Dorian traced.

But she shook her head, desperately holding on to who she was and unwilling yet to admit her strength. She and Dorian half carried Levi, as Thomas' power hit them full force.

They saw monsters moving, decaying. They leaped through space where frightening worlds spun out of control at them through the blackness. Stars came too close, burning them to crisps. They were reborn, felt life, only to burn up again.

They could not have escaped such powerful illusions if not for the Watcher growing on its own. The Watcher was Justice developing on a higher plane. While it knew its power, its source and its destiny, Justice did not. Not yet. But she now had gathered enough of its energy to break through Thomas' illusions to protect Levi. It was for her like taking a broom and sweeping away cobwebs.

204

Worlds and darkness, suns and free-fall gave way to the Quinella, where she and Dorian still stood in the heat clutching the weakened Levi between them. They were at the riverbank. Levi was alert; and, gently, they let him down to sit on it. His breath came in ragged sighs. His eyes were bright and feverish, and he did not perspire.

In the middle of the black river sat Thomas in water up to his neck. It was no illusion of him, although, blinking, Levi believed it was. Ever so carefully, Thomas lifted his arms out of the water. They glistened, black with leeches.

Floating toward them, they saw he had rolled up his pants legs and had taken off his shirt. Like one of his own nightmares, he stood up on shore, with his legs, arms and chest an evil of leeches, pulsating. Feeding on his blood.

Thomas grinned.

For it was Levi who felt the pain.

Levi began scooting over the dry bank, slapping at his arms and legs. Moaning, he struck at invisible leeches and let out short, piercing screeches.

Awful to hear in the hot, heavy stillness of the summer countryside.

You would do that to your own brother—give him the pain and not take it yourself? Justice traced to Thomas. The fearful sight of him covered with leeches turned her stomach.

He has the pain, so do something about it, Thomas traced to her. *Show me what you think you can do.*

If you don't stop it at once, I'll have *to show you,* she traced. Yet she dreaded the growing change, the becoming.

Thomas made no reply, but stood there, twenty feet from them, with leeches sucking at him. Levi grew visibly weaker. He had fallen on the ground, half unconscious;

moaning and twitching. It was the sight of him that caused Justice to overcome her dread. She knew what she must do.

For the Watcher was completing itself within her mind. At once, it knew she knew it was she.

She tasted fear. "Ahhh," escaped her lips, a sigh of resignation. She knew anguish. She understood the source and destiny of herself, Justice, the Watcher.

She knew her power.

Wavering motion. An enormous tremor of light and dark was her thinking, hugely magnified. Observing.

Thomas doubled over, picking at the leeches. At once, Levi stopped screaming. He lay still; then sat up. He was weak but calm now.

At first, Thomas wouldn't scream, wouldn't admit that Justice with her power had turned back the pain where it belonged. He fell, tearing leeches from his arms. It hurt him unbearably. "Justice!" he cried out, coughing, screaming: "I . . . I . . . o-only—g-g-get 'em off—guh-guh ooofff!"

Leeches appeared to combine in a flowing movement. They streamed down Thomas, making a pile at his feet. The pile rolled toward the water; it leaped in, as though a vacuum had sucked it under.

Thomas was flung about on the flat bank of the Quinella. He landed on one shoulder, on his back, as if someone had taken him by the arm and had hurled him. His face rubbed in the dust. Soon, he was caked with it from head to foot. He snorted, he coughed and spat, as dust filled his nostrils and coated his tongue.

The hard earth swirled into a dust devil as tall as Thomas. It lifted him higher than the shade trees. Up there, in the swirl of dust and air, he saw the day divided into yesterday, today and a day of future. In all moments, time flowed through continuously. What happened yesterday mattered today and would affect tomorrow.

Thomas was brought down again as quickly as he had been lifted up on high. Dust settled back to dry earth. Thomas stood, transfixed. Out of the air, a brittle branch came forth from the future. Sometime during yesterday, he had torn the very same branch from a tree. Today, it lay dying with its sap oozing into the ground. And tomorrow, it would become the dry, dead thing now poised before him.

The branch soundly thrashed him. It quit only when his legs and back showed welts. Thomas took the beating without flinching. He made no move to protect himself. Finally, the branch disappeared into thin air.

Only the sound of the Quinella waters, sluggish, slow ripples on the silence. Thomas panted heavily, his eyes on the ground. His skin oozed blood from the leeches and the thrashing. But he was a powerful, strong boy and he would heal, Justice knew.

So. Is it proved? Justice traced to Thomas. She opened the way for Levi to connect mentally with them. Dorian had already connected.

Silence, in which Thomas waited, hoping the red marks of the thrashing would fade from his body. But they were no illusion. They didn't disappear, nor did the pain. He gazed at Justice and down again. Truly, she had power, and he pondered the likelihood of her having more fabulous gifts.

Pausing to swallow once, he traced, *You've proven it. You win.*

It's a war between us, to win or lose? Justice traced back to him.

Bitterly: *I won't be second.*

Then you'll have to leave us, she traced.

When?

In the future.

You're sure it's me who'll have to leave? Thomas traced.

Well, it's you who won't be second, Justice traced. *Your choice today decides tomorrow.*

That's the way you *read it,* bitterly he traced again.

That's the way the future reads, believe me, Justice traced back. And then: *Come, Thomas, help us with Levi.*

Lee!

Thomas had completely forgotten his brother. Quickly, he crossed the space between them and, kneeling, gathered the weakened Levi in his arms. Thomas winced under the weight. His muscles flexed too tight and the leech and thrashing wounds oozed again. Still, he didn't falter. Gritting his teeth, he lifted his brother and carried him into the shade.

Justice was holding Thomas' shirt cradled in her arms. She and Dorian with their gifted hands had cleared a small area of water of pests and had wet the shirt. The liquid Justice wrung from the shirt into Levi's mouth was as fresh and clean as spring water.

Thomas couldn't remember a time when he had liked Justice much. Now, admitting her greater power, he knew they would never be close. Yet he did care about Levi. He had abused his brother. He had toyed with him, as a cat with a mouse. For all his cruelty—and Thomas knew he had been terribly cruel to Levi—there was still a part of him that would protect his brother. Regretfully, he would one day abandon Levi to his sister and Dorian, if Justice was to be believed. To think of leaving his identical behind, even in some far-off future, brought him a depth of sorrow that no singleton would understand.

Lee!

They had never known life without one another. They had been a world unto themselves.

Put him down here, Justice traced to Thomas.

He had carried Lee deep into the shade, avoiding snake nests at the edge of the low branches. He set Lee down with his back against the aged, thick trunk of a mighty buckeye tree whose shade held the scent of cool earth. Justice smoothed Lee's face with the shirt. Dorian removed his steaming tennis shoes and his socks. Levi smiled wanly at them as the coolness of shade brushed his toes.

"Feel better?" Justice asked, smiling at him.

"Much, much better," he said softly.

Lee! It was Thomas. Levi turned to look at him, his exhausted eyes locked on his brother's. As though looking into his own self, Levi saw anger—what didn't he see? He saw fear, pride, loneliness, a bit of caring. There was not to be seen a large amount of love in Thomas. But Levi knew that he cared, deep down and in his own way. Before Thomas could speak again in his mind, Levi took hold of his palm in a wordless handshake. It was enough.

Justice commanded Dorian and Thomas to take places against the tree.

The way Levi is sitting, she traced, *backs to the tree.*

Thomas was about to protest when he sensed something watching in his mind. He did as he was told.

On the opposite side of the tree from Levi, she traced to him. *Dorian, you on the opposite side from me, while I take the side facing the river.*

She reached out and clasped Thomas' hand on one side of her and Levi's on the other. They, in turn, clasped Dorian's hands. In this way, Justice's sentience—her power of observing and knowing through the senses—coursed its way through the four of them in an unbroken circle. They saw what she saw.

This, the first chance she'd had to reflect since self-awareness. She was set free in a space-time inner universe, at the heart of which was the Watcher of her power.

Explain how we have come to be this way, Thomas traced. His voice echoed through darkness. *Who are we?*

The first, Justice traced. *We four are the first unit. I'm the Watcher.*

And Dorian? Thomas traced.

He sensed a removal as Justice pulled herself back and pulled back the sensations that were Levi's. What remained were the selves of Thomas and Dorian. Thomas recognized himself. Then what was unhealthy within him drained away. His anger and hate poured out of him. What few physical ills he had were not serious, but were nonetheless soothed and repaired by Dorian.

Justice, with Levi, came forward again. She explained that it was her wish to add Dorian to their unit for obvious reasons.

But why us? Thomas persisted. *Why are* we *the first?*

We *aren't what's important,* she traced. *Someone, something is always "first." The first dawn, the first cellular creature. First people.*

Their alteration must have been an accident. The difference in one chromosome was enough to alter a few inherited characteristics. Into existence could come sensory and physical changes, the release of genetic information far beyond the ordinary.

Sentience. Telepathy. Telekinesis—motion produced without the use of force. And clairvoyance—ability to see objects or actions beyond the natural range. The four of

210

them each had one or more of these capacities. But Justice's power was exotic, giving her the energy to combine these forces.

Our place isn't here, Justice traced. *Our time isn't now, but in the future.*

Eyes closed, hands touching, the four of them were quite invisible, camouflaged as they were by the old shade tree.

In the future, we'll be too old and weak, Thomas traced.

We'll be just as we are now, Justice traced.

What?

I can get us there. Now, she traced.

While we're under this tree, we can be in the future, too? Thomas traced.

She traced no more. There was no need for her to.

Show me the future, at last, Thomas traced.

Justice sensed something disbelieving in his tone. *Do you wish just to see it,* she traced, *or do you want to go in it?*

There was stillness as Thomas thought this through. His excitement grew.

The way to the future has to be learned, she traced. *That will take time. But I can show you some of it.*

His anger flared. She knew the fierceness of his jealousy at her holding the balance of power.

Eyes closed, Thomas cringed at being so observed. There was no thought or feeling he could keep secret, joined as he was.

Dorian drained off Thomas' anger and brought him a soothing flow of infeeling.

It was at that moment that Levi had a sudden awareness. Their combined intelligence, the unit, revealed that the part of it called Dorian would in the future be known as Healer.

Justice commenced a minute tracing with Dorian as they

observed and searched Levi's system. The infeeling continued as Dorian drew away Levi's exhaustion, and as much of his illness as he was able.

Some moments later, inward time might have ended for all of them. The unit, the four of them, spread out into a vast, inner nothing where all tracing among them ceased. Thought and feeling hung suspended, as though life itself had closed down. The Watcher turned away from the present.

The unit heard voices rising. Out of nothing came babbling noise, a multitude of cries growing distant, vague, as from a time to come.

All at once, the unit opened its eyes and observed across the flowing river Quinella. It flicked its eyes from right to left. As it saw along the riverbank, it brought forth the future.

The unit moved its heads to see. It sat on a cliff edge, looking down. Far below and all around it was the future.

Thomas tore himself from the unit. He ripped his way into the vast nothing between times. He found joining as a unit unbearable and he came to, hurled backward by the violent force of his re-entry into now. Falling hard on his back, he rolled over and lay low, his eyes fixed on the tree where Justice and the boys still were joined, minds as well as hands. But now the Watcher began fading out of their eyes.

Thomas stayed in a crouch as Justice looked all around, finally focusing on him, six feet away from her.

Don't ever break contact like that again, she traced. *We could have lost you between times forever and ever.*

Who cares! You think I care? His tracing fairly screamed

at her: *I don't care! You won't turn me into some—unit! I won't be some kind of monster machine controlled by you!*

A person over there has to be joined, she traced. *Everything over there is a group, a joining. There's no other way to survive.*

I won't become a unit! Thomas traced furiously.

Then you won't survive!

Thomas was shaking all over, with his arms wrapped around himself, as though he thought he might fly away in tiny pieces.

She coaxed him back over to the tree, where the four of them grouped together again. Thomas hunched over under the heavy branches. He moaned softly, his face in his hands.

Levi took hold of his brother's shoulder. He didn't feel weak now or have pain of any kind. But he was tired and very sad inside.

"You wanted me to show you the future," Justice said to Thomas. "I even took you there. Not all the way in, not so you would be in danger, but partway, so you could see it and smell it, feel it and know it."

"I . . . IIII," Thomas began stuttering, and quickly entered her mind to trace: *Why can't we just stay here? We don't even have to use our power. I won't use it on anybody ever again, I promise. We've kept it a secret up until now. Why can't we just stay here? Or even help people, if you want. Who needs a unit!*

Thomas, don't you see? Justice traced. *We can't use it here.*

Before she had ceased tracing, Levi could certainly see that. Still connected to Justice's mind, he saw the problem they would face in the present. Grimly, he nodded. Glancing at Dorian, he found that he, too, had seen. He and Dorian accepted the unit she had made of them. Unquestionably, they knew she would never use it against them.

Justice sighed. Gazing at Thomas, she hated seeing the grief and despair he had not yet realized shone through his eyes.

"Thomas, we're the first," she said, attempting to explain. "And why we are isn't important now. We just are, so stop and think what that means. There are people who would give anything to control our power. There's no telling what they might do to us."

Thomas had already thought of this and he nodded agreement. *But you could stop anyone, Justice,* he traced.

Oh, maybe for a time, she traced. *But not forever. And the authorities would certainly get in on it. They'd want to take the four of us away someplace safe to study us.*

"But you don't have to go even that far," she said quietly. "Think about Mom and Dad. Think what it would be like for them to know their three kids—"

She broke off, aware that Thomas was feeling the overwhelming sadness she had already seen in his eyes.

"Thomas . . ."

I want . . . , he traced. *I . . . just want . . . to be the way we were. I want . . . I want to go home and see Mom and Dad.* His chest heaved up and down in a rush of emotion. His eyes filled, but he did not cry.

Justice touched him on the wrist, but soon drew her hand away. Thomas could recover by himself. He pulled himself in. They all did. Each remembering what this summer had been like. Thomas and Levi, age thirteen. Justice, age eleven. Dorian, thirteen in a couple of weeks. Themselves being kids. Their moms and dads.

At least Dorian's mom knows about us. Thomas traced what they all had been thinking. *She knows because*

214

she's . . . He didn't know what he should call Mrs. Jefferson.

She's a Sensitive, Justice traced. *She discovered my power and she helped me recognize it and use it sensibly. She'll help us, Thomas. She'll help get you over this part that's so sad.*

"I went through feeling that way yesterday," Justice told them. "I guess, all our lives, that kind of feeling of separation will come over us. That's why we have to stick together."

I still don't see how we can go to the future and remain right here, too, Thomas traced.

You saw a little of how it's done a few minutes ago, Justice traced. *And you saw what a shock going can be. We need Mrs. Jefferson to prepare you and Levi. Then Dorian and I will teach you the rest. But for now . . .*

She paused, telepathically checking on Levi to see if he had rested long enough.

I'm fine now, Levi traced. Yet he felt melancholy, as they all did. He was deeply shaken—they all were—to comprehend finally how different the four of them were from everyone else. They'd have to work hard to live with it. And he felt Justice's awareness agree with him.

But I won't be part of any unit, Thomas broke in on all of them, tracing to them all. *I'll be me, alone, if I have to. You wait and see.*

"Come on," Justice said to them. She would let Thomas believe what he liked.

Together, all of them left the protection of the shade trees. Stepping in the midst of writhing creatures, they found the day, the black river, everything, just as it had been—a heat-drenched day under a burning sky.

"The Great Snake Race is over and done," Justice said.

"And you won it," Dorian reminded her.

She didn't care to discuss winning and losing. But Thomas had overheard.

I had eighteen snakes, carefully he traced in their minds. *I could have won it, but that wouldn't've been fair to the other guys and Slick.* He gazed, unblinking, at Justice. Something of his old self shone through.

"Meaning," she said, "I shouldn't have won it because I'm your sister, I'm a relative. Well, I honestly didn't know that my snake was pregnant. I won it fair and square."

Thomas had to smile, they all did, when it flashed through their minds what a shock it had been seeing all those baby snakes.

"Eight-t-t-teen," Thomas said softly, and traced: *I come in second there, too.* He kicked his sneaker in the dirt.

Levi said, "I don't know how the two of you can go on so calmly about the snake race, with all that's happened." He looked troubled. "There's a lot we need to talk about. I mean, when we go to the future, do we have our bodies? And how are we supposed to act while we're here in the present? Do we use power only through the unit?"

Justice was looking at him as from a great distance.

Somewhere in him, and in all of them, was the Watcher, tracing, *Not to worry, Levi. Day by day, it will be dealt with.*

"Come on," Justice said to them. For a split second, her voice vibrated around them. When it ceased, all was still.

They started back. Thomas and Levi took the lead, while Justice brought up the rear with Dorian.

She was feeling very good. She was Justice. Not very big, age eleven. She was Justice, the Watcher. Given power because it was needed. Not now, but in another place and

216

time. She didn't mind it that she had been born in the wrong age. And she was content to be different as long as she was not alone. She would never be alone again.

They had started slowly through the high weeds. By the time they were over the fence, they were dripping with sweat. Wiping their wet hands on their pants legs and shirts, they picked up their bikes and hurried to be gone. Not Justice, not the others, gave a glance backward toward the Quinella Trace. Black-water river, they knew they would be seeing it and its future day upon day.

They were on their bikes, Thomas in the lead. Instantly, they raced in a flurry of shining, spinning wheels and glinting metal. Hollers, and grunting from the exertion of climbing hills too fast. They had nothing more on their minds than beating the heat across town. Fresh cold drinks of water. Of getting home.

Kids.